MW01181391

The Shattered Queen,
and Other New Mythologies

The Shattered Queen, and Other New Mythologies

A Short Story Collection
by
Jaym Gates

Falstaff Books
Charlotte, North Carolina

The Shattered Queen, and Other Mythologies
Copyright 2016 Jaym Gates

Licensed in the US by Falstaff Books, LLC. All stories contained herein are works of fiction. Any resemblance to actual people, places, or events is purely coincidental.

Cover Design: Galen Dara

Interior Design: Susan H. Roddey
www.shroddey.com

All rights reserved. No part of this book may be reproduced in any form by any electronic or mechanical means including photocopying, recording, or information storage and retrieval without permission in writing from the author.

All Rights Reserved.

ISBN-13: 978-1542523691
ISBN-10: 1542523699

Published by Falstaff Books 2016
Charlotte, North Carolina

www.falstaffbooks.com
Printed in U.S.A

Contents

First Dream

DARK WATER LAPS GENTLY against the raw soul. It has drifted alone for untold ages, the last fragment of a dead universe. It has fed on its own burned flesh to survive, eating the memories of the one it came from. Its dreams infuse the water. Some take form, islands of reality in a sea of possibility. Others drift on, or settle to the ocean's floor to be found in some distant era.

The water laps against the soul again, as though to wake it. It draws some few dreams to cluster around the soul. They take form, building a body long and strange. It is nothing that has been seen before, but well-suited to this primeval sea.

It drifts more purposefully through the water now, reassembling its memories.

It remembers a great light, and a wall of bones, a scorched plain and a whispering library.

It remembers…

Dreams Before

WHEN I WAS A CHILD, my mother told me stories of the ones who came before. Dragons who sang the world to shape, queens who spoke with the voice of prophecy and raised nations from their dreams, heroes who stood against the tides of history. All these stories she told me, and more, through the burning hours when the white light washed over the walls at the edge of the world. To venture outside during that time was to be burned alive, the flickering light of a slow-dying supernova lashing against the black sands.

She told me that time turns the same as the world, that what once was will be again. Her eyes, burned white by exposure to the light, stared wistfully into the distance, looking for the future, she always said. I asked her how people could have been so mighty. Our women were not queens, we had no heroes, and the dragons had turned to stone and worn to sand before I was born.

They forgot to dream, she said, wistfully. *The world burned, and they could not sleep for the light.*

When Nothing Was

I SIT AT THE END of the world and watch it fade. The stars are falling into my hands, mingling with my tears. They stain my fingers, a fantastic palette of wishes and dreams. I dabble with them, drawing their hopes and memories on my cheeks, my breasts, nonsense patterns. Trying to make sense of what is happening.

I am out of skin to paint, but the memories continue. I fling the clinging stars at the dark sky, but the ink slithers like a living thing, refusing to become a picture. Droplets hang in the air, turn to fine mist. Fine mist streams into nothing. I need to hold together my world, but I can't. It is falling away from me, drifting into nothing, devoured as quickly as it is born.

I sit at the end of the world, at the place where time ends and infinity begins. I sit with my brushes and my ink, my stardust and my tears. I sit at the end of the world and watch the lightning play with discarded memories. I sit and paint nonsense memoirs on broken stone until even that is pulled out of my hands.

I stand on the last stone and stare into the void. Around me, the destruction is singing, a lonely and discordant keen. I sing with it, the words pattering into the dark, casting a line into the pool to see what bites, but nothing does. All that comes back is silence.

The stone path I was following is disintegrating, gravel, dust, gone. In front of me, the world falls away, behind me is...nothing. Everything is gone, and now the ends are vanishing, too. I wonder if there is an end to the ending, if I too will crumble into dust and nothingness, or if I will linger here when everything is gone, floating through empty space.

I sit at the end of the world and remember, but the memories are fading. Infinity is reaching into my head, stealing my thoughts, eating them, licking its fingers clean of my grief and love. I wonder, maybe, if the emptiness is lonely, or if, from the other side, I am reforming, reaching back to try and piece myself together. The memories unspool before my eyes, and I reach out, as if I can hold them to me. Instead, my flesh joins them, pulling loose from brittle bones.

It does not matter. Grief is beautiful, floating in gossamer streams from my eyes and lips. Harsh love falls through my hands like sand through an hourglass. Hope dissipates, mist on a hot morning. Joy, aged and silver with wisdom, wraps me in its embrace and lays me out under its shroud. My brush falls from senseless fingers; lassitude pours through me as though a lover's gentle hand has brought me here. My gaze dims, filled with mist and dust.

I am here, and all things come to an end, an end that is beautiful and gentle. Here is peace, where hurt does not leave tracks in the white dust, and the mist is undisturbed by suspicious eyes.

But even the end is ending. I am propelled forward. Fury and joy surge through limp limbs, bearing me to the surface, drowning me in knowledge

The darkness rebuilds me, sleek and mysterious. Eyes and ears and lips, hands forming from the ashes of stars. I dip my fingers in starlight and begin to paint, silver shadows in the night. One line at a time, one dot, one smear. Slowly it begins to hold. I am painting faster than it can be eaten away.

Words fill my empty mouth. I am singing. I don't know the song; I don't know the language. Maybe I am singing a lost song, maybe a new song. My voice slips from my lips and dances through the sky.

My paintings take new form, rising with their own lives, a strange new world building around me, evolving and beautiful, strange as the dreams in my dead heart.

It is beyond me now, my little paintings pulsing with their own wild life.

I sit at the beginning of the world and look at a new thing. A new world. My pictures and my songs are growing. Light shimmers in the steps I took, sweeps in a stately memory-dance. Voices call in the darkness, bodies build around them. My memoirs are their memories, my songs are their voices, my paintings are their lives. I watch my dreams grow, filling this new world with laughter and joy and hope.

I sit at the beginning of the world, at the place where time begins, where infinity takes shape. I sit with my brushes and my ink. I sit and paint a new world.

I am nothing, but around me...

...around me is everything.

The Gift of the Child to the Mother Mountains

THE LAST LIGHT OF the sun glints gold on the King's beard, the first light of the moon highlights his wife's sharp bones.

The Queen leans forward, her eyes cool. Silver Tongue is her name, and the minstrels of a thousand worlds still sing of her battle with the white wolves of the Cloud Kings. She has ruled this land for many decades, but age has not dimmed her sight nor weakened her arm.

She signs something to her herald—her voice is too beautiful to be heard, a single world will break the foundations of a city, a sentence could shatter castles. The herald turns pompously to the thin woman standing before the thrones.

"Name your titles and your mission," he demands.

"I have no titles," she says softly, and there is a disappointed exhale from the crowd. There is no thunder in her voice; the palace does not shake. What hero this scrawny thing? "My claim to this quest is that all others have failed, and I am the last hero in the land."

Angry muttering from the perimeter of the throne room does not herald good things for the young woman. Perhaps the age of the great quests is over; perhaps the Concubines of the Phoenix offer richer rewards. But they are heroes still. Whether or not there is money, or fame, in a task does not matter. Their names are their souls; their titles are their lives.

"What is your name, Child?" asks Great Beard. Twilight gathers around the tower, though night long since fell everywhere else.

The vast shadow cast by Great Beard and the tall, severe shaft of his wife's shadow swallow the young hero whole.

"I have not yet earned a name, sire," she says, and blushes, but does not raise her eyes. "I am no great thing yet."

A Child, a nameless creature, to unmask them with a few words? No.

"Explain." And the herald's command is not to be denied.

"*Heroes have no names and monsters have no hands. Kings have no ears and Queens have no faces. Slaves have no souls and peasants have no voices.*" She chants ly. The naming spell, the foundation of the world. The beginning , the laws laid down by the Three Mothers when they shaped this ~~w...~~ he one that was.

"These are named. Faced. Hands and souls, they have it all. That is why we are fading. Your peace is killing us. We are human again, not Children. We have resigned our power to the pages of mouldering books."

"A presumptuous claim for you to make. And you say that you will ask for nothing?" asks Great Beard.

"If I return, I shall be content in having completed a task that no one else could."

"All legends begin somewhere," Great Beard says, and his voice is kind. "Many great heroes have tried, and have failed. Should you succeed, what reward will you seek to claim?"

"No reward, sire. I ask only for the chance to do that which has been denied me before."

Yes, signs Silver Tongue. *She is the one.*

Great Beard considers it, weighing the thing before him with the task ahead. "Then so be it. I cannot name you, by your own rules, so you will not receive the power of our people's voice. Go forth, Child, and prove that we are not yet a dead race."

It is dawn, below. Dusk, above.

The tower stretches beyond the reach of the sun, holding the sky and sun apart. Child stands at the gates of the tower, ragged and plain and alone. The other heroes are gone, with their names and their fine horses and their jeweled, magic swords. Child stands in front of the King and Queen and their Children, her body lean, scarred, and boyish. A clean but plain sword hangs on her back along with a bedroll and a pouch of food. That is all she has in this world, all she has to save the people of the Three Mothers from themselves.

"You have no horse?" Great Beard asks. "No magic sword?"

"A hero does not need these things."

Silver Tongue holds a strange device to her lips and speaks for the first time, her words mechanical and hurtful to the ears, but the world does not break.

"Perhaps not, but it is the Queen's right to grant a boon to aid you in your way."

Child bows. "I would be most honored and pleased."

"I will give you horse or sword," she says, smiling coldly. Her gifts are legendary. Swords forged by her brothers, so mighty that no man can wield them; horses from the gates of hell, so terrible and swift that no man can ride them without her blessing; bows that can shoot the moon from the sky, can a man but draw them. Each comes with a price, and a burden. The Queen's Gift is not of kindness, nor charity.

"Bring me the Wolf Tooth," says Silver-Tongue, turning to the King's captain. He bowed to her and left.

She looks at Child, and her words are not without sympathy. "If you can master this sword and lift it, then it will be yours till the end of your days, and it will bring you many dark gifts. If you cannot…then perhaps you will find worth some other place."

Six men carry the sword between them in a net of silken rope. Their muscles knot and sweat runs down their faces. The sword would not draw a second glance in the market; it is without ornamentation or cunning device.

"Lift it, and it is yours," says Silver Tongue.

Child leans over it, staring at the ugly blade. Oily grey-black metal shivers gently under her regard, the vibration strong enough to shove the sword-slaves off their feet. The sword slams into the earth, shattering the stone of the courtyard.

"This is your own sword?" Child's hand hovers over it, reverently. "She has the sharp tongue of a forgotten maiden and her deeds sing from her blade."

"I have slain dragons with her, and trolls, and kings," Silver Tongue answers, softly. "My killing-time is past, and she must have new blood, or she will find it where she can."

Child lays her hands on the sword, and the bitter cold of the steppes thrusts into her blood. Burning, freezing, mad with pain. But she holds it, wraps her hands around its hilt, listens to the song of a wild thing caught in steel. It is a melody that calls to the coldness of her blood, to tales of dark forests filled with wolves. There is no golden dawn in these dreams, no fair prince or lovely maiden. The sword promises her blood and pain, long, dark nights and lonely trails.

The blade promises her all of these things, and her heart pounds at the thought, for it reads her darkest dreams and brings them to life.

"Yes," she whispers. She does not think of the Watchers, of the men who have toiled to lift this ugly sword. The stern Queen does not loom over her anymore. She, the hero, takes the weapon in her hands and raises it to the memory of the deep forests and silent predators with a war-cry from some other time or place or throat.

The echoes still rebound from the walls when the spell fades and awareness returns. Deep embarrassment cloaks her, and she seems to shrink back into herself.

"You have been chosen," says Silver Tongue, and the Named are silent as the sword molds itself to its new mistress's dreams. A moment, and the ugly grey thing is gone, replaced with a light, long blade the color of forest shadows.

Child brings the sword close and caresses the black hilt. Her hand fits perfectly along the body of the running wolf that is flowing into the grip, thorny branches forming a guard around her fingers.

"I am chosen," she says, and bows to the Queen. "I am ready."

"Wait," cries one of Silver Tongue's daughters. Tall and dark like her mother, she is the eldest and fairest of the four. Though she has never desired to wield a sword, she stands at her father's left hand and learns her mother's secrets. She is Far-Eyes, the next Queen, and it is her right to grant a Queen's favor as well, for she is already of power to rival her ancestors.

"I would grant my favor to the hero."

Silver Tongue inclines her head. "You may indeed grant favor or gift."

"I would grant the hero a steed that she may complete her task quickly and restore my father's line to their glory."

"That is your right," says the Queen, "and you may choose any horse in the stables."

But, instead, the woman steps forward and takes Child's hand, pressing a small stone into her palm.

"Take this," she says, "and when you come to the Burning Rocks, kneel in the center of them and chant the words *exen, gransit, baryiv, cranhg* three times. Your steed will come to you there."

Child bows, deeply. "You honor me, lady," she says, and kisses Far-Eyes' palm. She is not immune to the woman's beauty or presence, and Silver Tongue's eyes narrow in interested speculation, but she bides her time.

"Farewell, hero," says Great Beard, and his guards heave open the gates of the tower.

The way to the Burning Rocks is easy enough, beset only with the nuisances that any common traveler would face. Child makes good time through the gentle hills and valleys, until she comes to the edge of the world of Three Mothers, to the lands where the Blood did not fall. Men are not strange here; women are not blessed.

But even here, the land is touched. Hungry things haunt the bright hours of the day, and the darkness consumes unwary prey at night. It bleeds from her homeland, and even the weakest thread is enough to twist the land. As she walks, the ground grows hot beneath her feet. The Burning Rocks are said to be the embers of a god's fire, having smoldered through the centuries and that only the final rain will douse them out (more dour postulates think it to be left over from one of the infrequent cleanings of Fire-Skin's commode).

Whatever the cause, Child sits down in a clearing between the rocks and chants *exen, gransit, baryiv, cranhg.*

Sweat pours from her face and body. Her clothes catch fire and burn from her body. The heat sears her skin, beats the air from her lungs.

Exen, gransit, baryiv, cranhg.

Her short hair is singed, the acrid stench catching on her tongue.

Exen, gransit, baryiv, cranhg! She cries the last incantation and dashes the charm to the ground.

The earth splits underneath her. Fire shoots into the sky, red and liquid as a geyser.

From the rift rise twitching red ears wreathed in flame. Clopping slowly up the broken banks comes one of Fire-Skin's younger children. The body of a horse perched on cat's paws, heavy antlers branching from his high-set head, the steed hauls himself into the upper earth and snorts. Mucus spatters on Child's skin and she yelps. Three tiny burns mark her upper arm, perfect circles.

The rift closes behind the creature. Child straps her pack and sword to her back and approaches the animal cautiously. Flames wreath the animal's body. How is she supposed to ride this thing?

The steed tosses his head, dancing closer to her and presenting his back.

There is nothing else to it. Child grabs the thick strands of the steed's mane and hauls herself onto his back.

Like living roots, his mane curls around her hands. The flames enfold her thighs, singing her flesh. The stallion bolts, snorting fire and brimstone.

Child remembers the tales that her mother told her about how the people of the high steppes tamed their mounts, full grown mares and stallions. She remembers the darker, more sinister tales of what happened if a mount such as this was not brought to bridle quickly.

She has only a length of stout, twisted rope hanging from her pack. Wrenching a hand free from the prison of mane, she gropes wildly behind her, slithering about on the horse's back. Perhaps sensing her purpose, he speeds into a sharp right-hand turn, forcing her to grab his mane again.

He zigs and zags, though he never tries to throw her, merely keep her off balance. Once she discovers his plan, she ignores his wild course. His next turn nearly does throw her, but she does not grab on, and he corrects quickly, keeping her on his back. She is to be lunch, and he does not want to lose her.

She finally grabs the rope and yanks her other hand out of his mane. Forming a loop, she checks that it will slip easily and bends low over his neck. He spins in his tracks, forcing her to cling for dear life. His mane no longer clutches at her hands, and the fires roar hotly enough to singe her skin black.

He has guessed her purpose, and now, between captivity and flight, he makes his choice. Muscles tightening in his back, he leaps into the air, twisting. It is too late.

Child pulls the noose over the steed's nose, catching it on the bony ridges and spurs. Leaning on it, drawing it tight, she leans back and hauls on his nose as he goes bucking and twisting off across the uneven ground.

Her hands are raw and bleeding, her skin scorched and her hair burned away by the time the steed is tamed. He comes to a halt, his sides heaving. Yet there is no defeat in his proud stance, only acceptance. He is, after all, shaped from the fires for the lords of the Hellfire. Such beasts do not know defeat.

She looks around at the towering rocks, at the blackness of the place, and knows that she has brought him to hand in the barest window of remaining time. The Seared Lands drop into the God's Mouth, sheer cliffs over the flaming pits, and nothing that enters will leave intact.

She had never been here.

"Where is Old Mother-Mountain?" she wonders aloud.

The steed pricks his ears and takes off at a right angle to his previous path, picking his way through the fire-swept wastelands.

As the days wear on, Child comes to appreciate the Princess's gift more even than the Queen's. The horse—she knows no other name for his species, for she knows of no one who has seen one of these ferocious beasts in the flesh—never loses his way. After the first day, he stops fighting her. Though they are still in the Wastelands, she stops on the second day near a fetid river, desperate for relief.

Every movement is agony. The horse's slick black flesh—as smooth and hairless as obsidian—has burned away most of the skin from her naked thighs. Though he seems to cool as they moved farther away from the Burning Rocks, she does not wish to sacrifice her only other clothes, and grits her teeth against the agony.

So she stops him beside the shallow water and falls from his back, the rope in her burned hands, hoping that this does not give him his freedom back. The sharp rocks and rough sand of the river meet her, fold her in their embrace, and tear the rope from her nerveless fingers. Slamming, tumbling, snatching, the current thrusts her down the stream, and though there had been no ripples visible, pulls her under, grinds her face into the gossip-sharp rocks. Cold water eddies with scalding hot. She cannot move her limbs for the pain and fear.

It is all around her. Beneath her, unforgiving ground. Above her, malicious water. It pushes down her throat and wraps its hand around her face. Child has faced fear before; she has fought and overcome.

Now, she is over-matched. Wailing and struggling, she is batted this way and that. Skin cracks and peels off in crispy sheets as burned limbs force themselves to new angles. The grey water runs red. Dead skin sticks to her face, slimy, clinging. She sucks in a piece with the water that is filling her lungs and chokes, gagging, coughing.

In that moment, as her own body turns against her, she loses the battle. She stops fighting the current. Her limbs go limp in the deepening water. Lungs fill.

Welcome, child, says a thin, crackling voice. *Welcome to my kingdom. My son has done well.*

Fire-Skin. Child's eyes open, and she is lying in the river still, face-up, the skin of water parting over the tip of her nose. So close. So far.

Against the wall, a great, naked figure stands silently, watching her. She meets the blank eyes without fear. "Fire-Skin."

Her voice is a croak, a tremor, a water-soaked gurgle. Coughs wrack her frame again, spewing a black sludge of skin and sand.

That is only my servant, Wildfire, says the voice. *I do not have form. I do not have shape. I cannot touch. Have you forgotten your gods already, little hero?*

"The gods have never done anything for me. Why should I learn of them when they are mere myth and legend?"

You are a hero. We have done things for you since before your birth. Since before your mother's birth, or her mother's. To be a hero is to be our youngest child, our form-while-waking. It would do well for you to learn some respect, brat, lest we take your disloyalty seriously.

"I do not want to be your form," she says, and struggles to sit, to move, to escape the drowning. "I want to be my own form."

Yet you lie there, in your own dying shell, in a pool of human filth. You lie there and decry all that we are, but you will not rise to help yourself.

"I am dying! My flesh is seared away; my limbs are broken. Your teeth have gouged out my flesh to feast on. I cannot rise, you hold me chained in my filth and pain."

I do not hold any chains, says the great voice, and the crackling deepens. *If you do not seek my help, then wake and help yourself. But you please me, Child, for you are not like the Children which my brothers and sisters bless. You have no sense of self-preservation, no fear of being stupid. As a token of my favor, you will rise in the armor of my breath, and my Child shall bear you wherever you wish to go, whether to the sky, or to the bowels of the earth.*

"What must I do for this gift?" She is bitter, spitting out the word 'gift'. Gifts came with price, and she had nothing left to pay.

You will make love to Wildfire. Her King has turned to the humans and runs from her passion. Her touch will change your flesh, and no sword shall ever piece it. Her breath will be in your lungs, and no cold shall ever shake you. Her power shall be in your voice, and none shall deny you.

And the air thickens with smoke, but the voice is gone, and the weightlessness, leaving Child floating in that pool that had been pulled from somewhere else.

The tall flame detaches itself from the wall and comes to her. Fire drips from the creature's fingers; great wings flare from her shoulders. Sparks burn in the black caverns of her eyes, and her lips are the red slash of a tree-trunk eaten from the inside by fire, the outside charred black. The creature is speaking to herself.

She reaches into the pool and wraps her hands around Child. Steam rises in billowing clouds, until Child cries out again, certain that she cannot not bear more pain. Wildfire's hands are gentle and feeling returns to the melted flesh of her legs.

"All that you must do, if you cannot bear my touch more, is cry *enough,* and I shall set you back in the pool to reawaken in your world," says Wildfire. Sparks fly from her lips when she speaks.

"You are a Queen," says Child, touching the blankness of Wildfire's face, where only the cavernous eyes and cracked mouth break the expanse of fire. "Why do you bend to me?"

"I am a Queen," agrees Wildfire, "and my Lord of the Forest has hidden behind the humans for many long years. There is no one to love me now."

"I will love you," says Child, "and be glad of it."

She kisses Wildfire and falls into the story of those lips.

The room fades away, turning into a towering forest. Coals lie in drifts over the earth, soot smudging the trunks of the ancient, towering trees. Above them, smoke has withered some green leaves, but the rest still shine brightly, high against the blinding blue sky.

Child's feet sink into the drifts, cause them to eddy like snow. Tiny tongues of flame lick at her calves, twine about her legs, crawl up her thighs. Wildfire's voice echoes through the trees, a wild song of delight. Beyond her, the red, the gold, black and orange of destruction laps forward like a hungry tide. Behind Child, the late-summer stretches into the mountains, gold and green and blue. But Wildfire stands in stark, mad beauty, a fusion of both horizons. Blue wreaths her body, glints from her broad shoulders and full breasts. White flickers between her thighs and at the ends of her fingers.

No hair crowns her head, only living flame dances and cascades around her as she steps out of the coals and catches Child in her arms. "I will love you fair," she says, "and as gently as I may."

"Do not be gentle," whispers Child, and presses her lips to one white-hot nipple.

Wildfire's laugh starts low, rumbling in the ground, and grows into a roaring, joyous tumult of pleasure as she throws her head back and twirls Child about her, wrapping both of them in a column of white fire.

"You are indeed blessed," she says, "and courageous. I will pull back the softness of the world and wrap you in strength."

Wildfire takes Child's face between her hands, scalding the still-wet skin. Child is not inexperienced; she has stayed in many a tavern and availed herself of the women available. But never has one done it with such intent and skill.

Child loses herself in the wild-woman's embrace. Wildfire is all around her, devouring her mouth, licking her thighs. Hands on her breasts and a firm pressure on her back, holding her up, hands stroking her face and parting her thighs. Too many hands, too few, not enough. The fire is in her blood now, every nerve screaming *enough, enough*! The pain is beyond anything she has known, yet it wakes a deep and hungry need for more.

Her own hands slip and float through the shifting body, drenched in fire. She has no thought but her own pleasure and that of her lover. The pain builds to unimaginable levels, until she wants to scream for it. Forward, forward, she immerses herself in Wildfire and breathes in the smoke. Her blood burns clean, her nightmares fade before the all-consuming light. The pain breaks away from her in a great wave and she is swept away on still greater pleasure.

"Is it too much?" asks Wildfire, only once. She is kissing Child's hand, stripping away the skin, the dead, black, dying skin with her teeth. "Do you wish to return?"

"Never," gasps Child, belly aching and legs weak. "It is not enough."

Wildfire, on her knees, presses her lips against Child's palm and leaves a searing kiss. She smiles up at her lover, sparks dancing in her eyes.

"Then I will show you the depths of the fire."

Wildfire stands. Wings, curling like hot strips of wood, spread from her back and cling to the branches of the trees around them. Holding out her hands to Child, she pulls the woman against her body.

"It is time to die," she says, "die in my arms and rise again to your new self."

"Gladly," replies Child, kissing the hollow of her lover's throat.

14

Wildfire bears her to the earth, and her wings come down to cover them.

Weightless, as though in the pool again. Bodiless, a flickering outline defined and drawn by Wildfire's touch. Mindless, captured and tormented with the ultimate, delicate dance of pleasure and pain. She has lost herself, and hot, wet darkness flows over her, stifles her.

The world falls away, and Child is limp in Wildfire's arms, lost in the darkness.

"Sleep," says the Queen, and lays herself gently over Child's inert body, feasting on the burning flesh. Each bitten place fills with glossy new flesh, as dark as volcanic glass. As the day wheels above them and turns to fire-lit night, Wildfire slowly rebuilds her lover.

She finishes, moments before dawn, and presses her face and hands to the ashy earth. "It is done, Mother," she says. "Give me your breath."

My breath will flow through you, but you must set her back to Bright World before she wakes. If she returns to you, you may keep her, but she must complete her quest first.

"She is the only one who has ever loved me. I want to keep her."

She has her own paths to tread, her own battles to face. It is the newest Age of Heroes, and she will be its mother.

Wildfire looks down into Child's proud face, utterly still and cast now in black glass. Her fingers, leeched now of some of their heat, stroke the slick cheekbones and lips.

"I will do as you command, Mother," she says, and scoops Child back into her arms.

Child floats in darkness, at rest, at peace. The delicious heat of her lover still encompasses her and she has no wish to leave.

Words flow around her, crackling and commanding. "Wake, little lover."

"No," moans Child, and tries to burrow back into the comforting dark.

"Wake," says Wildfire again, and there is sadness and teasing mingled in her voice. "Wake. You must complete your quest."

Slowly Child wakes. The world shifts around her, bright light spearing her eyes. The heat lingers in her veins. "I am awake."

"Good." Wildfire holds a stone cup in her hands. Fire plays along the rim, and something dark sloshes inside, steaming.

"You have been remade with my ashes and my blood, formed in my embrace," she says, kissing Child. "The breath of my Mother is in your lungs. You are blessed, and no weapon shall ever slay you."

"I thank you," says Child, closing her aching eyes. "What is in the cup?"

"It is my essence," replies Wildfire. "For though you live and are fleshed, blood does not yet fill your veins. Drink this, and your limbs will come to life." Wildfire cups her hand against Child's lips and pours the liquid into her mouth.

The unmistakable taste of Wildfire fills her mouth. Earth and ash, blood and incense, the deep musk of a sated woman. "This is not all blood," Child says when she can breathe again.

Sparks dance in Wildfire's eyes. "No, it is not. I want you to remember me, and I want to remember you."

"I do not think that there is any danger of that," says Child, and licks Wildfire's wet fingers.

Child now wears the same skin as the stallion, who no longer burns her. Child rides him hard through the last of the Wastelands until they come to the hills beneath the mountains. Nothing stands before her, all would-be challengers fading into the shadows at her approach.

The lands here are weird and dangerous, and Child finds reason to be grateful to Silver Tongue for her sword, and Wildfire for her armor. This is the land of Razor-Teeth, hungriest of the Mothers. Though she sits, hunched, on the northern plains, brooding over the tribes, her eyes do not miss anything that happens in her realm. Birds and beasts do not go near her, for her appetite is legendary. She guards the north, keeping the fell and ice-broken demons of the equator from overwhelming the rich lands there, but her price is steep.

Child can see her now, a looming, stoop-shouldered lump on the horizon. Head and shoulders above the great mountains around her, the Mother is a monolith of stone, clouds catching around her ears. Child would rather not go near her, but if anyone knows what is devouring the world, it will be Razor-Teeth.

Three more days pass before Child comes to the stretch of bare earth around the Mother. The Mother's great legs are crossed, her large hands folded over her belly. The ground shakes gently from her snoring, and snow clusters on her shoulders. She has not awakened for some time and will be terribly hungry when she does. Poor timing for a visit.

"How am I to get to her?" Child asks her steed. "She cannot hear me from here, surely, and I cannot climb, for she is too smooth."

The horse snorts and dances, tossing his head. There are legends about his kind, about them slipping skin and flesh, changing forms, wings and gills and all manner of strange things. But she had never heard more than legends even of his existence, before she summoned him.

"Fly," she says, "take me to her shoulder."

She grips hard at his mane, afraid, but he only kneels. Frustrated, she steps off. "Do you need a rest, oh tireless one?" she mocks, putting her pack on the ground.

He changes in front of her. His shoulders and front legs bow, twist, pull. Loud popping sounds turn her stomach as his limbs reform. His skin splits, stretching from leg and shoulder. Bones rise, crack, knit. Muscles knot over the bones, dripping blood.

And then, balancing on his dripping hind legs, the stallion grows his wings.

Awe fills her again as the creature carefully sidles towards her, wings billowing to keep his balance. His hide does not grow over the framework, they are raw flesh leaking burning blood, and it lends him a gruesome magnificence.

Even she is uncertain as to the wisdom of this, but carefully pulls herself onto his back, wrapping her legs around his sides. Screaming, he launches into the air.

At first, he is erratic, but his wings harden, stop growing, and he flies smoothly upwards.

The earth falls away from them, and storms threaten to the west, great banks of darkness piling up against the mountains. The wind, erratic and noisome, whines and gnaws at her hard flesh.

Child crouches against her mount's back and holds on as they draw near to the Mother-Mountain's eyes. Watching the skies thin, her blood runs cold in fear and wonder.

The Mother's wrinkles stand out in knife-edged relief, vast canyons carved across the landscape of her naked belly and breasts. Her eyes glitter like diamonds, set deep within cavernous sockets. They focus somewhere in the distance, contemplating the horizon. Stained teeth jut from the Mother's jaw, ragged and eroded. The snoring has stopped. The Mother is awake.

Child wonders at the geology, the physiology, of the Mother-Mountain. Wonders if the Mother can still move, or if she is locked in an endless pose of contemplation.

Great eyes snap into focus and home in on Child.

"Who are you?" says the Mother-Mountain, and the shock of her breath sends the steed tumbling through the air.

Child clings to him until he rights himself. Her heart pounding, she soothes him and presses him back towards the Mother, out of the direct line of her breath.

"I come on behalf of the God-Son King Great Beard and his Queen, Silver Tongue!" she screams above the gales. "Something devours the greatness of the world, leeches the strength from our arms, and renders us mute. We are becoming as mortals, and the light gathers because we are too weak to hold it back."

Razor-Teeth shrugs. The Mothers are not known for caring what their Children do. The Children were created to hold back the light when the Mothers grew weary, and if they fail, well, the Mothers did their part.

"I care not what silliness you Children have gotten yourself into. We gave you all you needed to hold back the light."

"And then you left us! You did not tell us how to use it, or what would happen if we let our darkness fade!"

Razor-Teeth shrugs. "It is still none of my concern. But the history of the universe is written in my bones. Look, if you have the courage to venture within."

Fire fills Child's veins. She does not fear the Mother-Mountain, though legends of her hunger fill human histories. She guides the steed to the Mother-Mountain's vast, bony shoulder. He lands, clinging to the rocks with his claws, and she leaves her pack and sword with him. She takes only a coil of rope, her knives, food, and some water.

Though the Mother appears smooth from a distance, her neck is covered with erosion and outcroppings and heavy wrinkles. Below, the wrinkles are too thick to help her, but here, the fine lines give her enough to use to climb. A few hairs sprout as well, thick as the pine trunks of Hirshia.

So she climbs, and the shoulder and the world fall away from her. There is only the skin in front of her, the next crevice; the eventual promise of the Mother's mouth keeps her going. Strangely soft, like slightly-warm lava, the skin gives way to her fingers.

Finally, she crests the neck, below the immense ear. She can see the wrinkled lips to her left, but the skin of the Mother's cheek is far smoother, and night is falling again. Weakness fills even her hardened limbs. Thunder rumbles behind the Mother's head, and Child gives up thought of reaching the mouth this night. Instead, she climbs into the Mother's ear and curls up into a tight little ball, imagining Wildfire's touch as the rain falls.

The sun rises early here, high above the clouds to strike prisms in the Mother's eyes. Child sets out in the crisp, cold morning, hoping that ice has not formed overnight.

Indeed, it has, but the heat of her body melts it. She eventually works her way to the Mother's lower lip. Her fingers slip. Flailing, she jams her fingers into the Mother's chin and scrambles onto the lip.

A wizened old man awaits her. "Welcome to the archives," he says, and ushers her into the shadowed cavern.

Sunspots burst in front of Child's eyes, slow to adjust to the dimness. Torches gutter, high on the slick walls, fizzling from drops of saliva. Immense, stained hulks of bone shine dully. The ground shifts ahead of her, throwing her off balance, and Child gasps as the outlines of a massive, grey tongue slowly appear, stretching off into the darkness.

"Welcome to the library," says the old man, cackling. "Now then, what do you want to know?"

"I seek a way to restore the might of the God-Sons and the Children of Darkness so that we may hold back the light a little longer," says Child.

"Ah, yes. You'll want Knife-Fingers for that," says the old man.

"Where would I find Knife-Fingers? I have never heard more than rumor of her passing."

The librarian shrugs. "Who knows? The teeth will tell."

"I cannot read," admits Child, her voice quiet and shamed.

"I know," says the librarian. He takes Child's arm and leads her to the first tooth. "But you do not need to read this history." He places her hand on the great mountain of ivory and points upward. "Words are not the only way to tell a story."

As a child, Child had heard many songs sung, and always, they wrote themselves to her mind, vast etchings of strange shapes and ideas. Now, looking at the stained histories, those same lines spread across the ivory. Upwards and outwards, more than the eye can see. She leans backward, her spine curving in an attempt to follow the melodies.

"Careful, child." The librarian taps the vast, fleshy floor with his stick. "You have woken her, and she is hungry. She will not care if you catch between her teeth."

Child totters and nearly falls as the floor roils under her feet. Thousands of songs unfurl in front of her, echoing in her ears and burning behind her eyes.

"Every cell in the universe is recorded here," says the librarian. "Every rock, every human, every beast. Each has a song the size of their deeds. You need only look at the beginning to find the Mothers and follow their threads until you find their latest notes."

"I could listen for three months and not come to the end! Why can't I start at the latest one?"

"The songs are not linear, and hers has dwindled over the centuries," he says.

"I shall be old and frail," frets Child.

The librarian smiles and claps his hands. "If you cannot abide a little time then of what worth is your quest?"

She has no answer for him, and so he chucks her under the chin and whistles through teeth as etched as the Mother's.

A trill above, and a pretty, cunningly-wrought bird wings down from dark heights. Sinew and metal gears, muscle and silk thread, wood skin and ivory feathers seem to grow in organic, undirected shapes, yet the whole is pleasing the eye and glittering with pale jewels. Sapphire eyes regard her curiously from a golden face.

"Mortals would lose their way among the songs and never return," says the librarian. "The bird will follow the one song without deviation."

"Why do you not offer him to everyone who comes?"

"Everyone?" There is a curious lilt, a tilt, as if the librarian has spent too much time around the bird. "Mortals do not come here often. You are the first. Rumors of us have...spread far. Only hunters, heroes, killers."

"I am a hero."

"You are not a killer."

20

She cannot refute that, so she is silent and listens to the damp sounds of the mouth and the click-whir-chirp-clink-hiss of the bird.

The librarian strokes three feathers, which spring from the bird's neck, dark among the light. "Cling fast to his back and empty your mind. The song will sing itself to you." He hands her a contraption of leather, eroded copper, bits of glass and feathers, and dangling stones. "Place this over your eyes, and you will see more clearly."

Slips of glass dangle over her eyes, red and gold and blue, painted and stained, beach-tumbled and church-glossed. The world shifts through their restless perspective. Beasts crawl out of the shadows while a worm eats a channel through the librarian's face. The bird quivers, a pile of feathers and ugly, rusted metal, yet it is whole and gleaming with newness.

"Do not think on it," says a brightly-colored voice near Child's ear. Echoes of his words shatter on the glass and tumble through her hands, incomprehensible. She throws her leg over the bird's saddle and clings as it launches into the air, far smoother than the horse-beast.

Wind whistles and flutes through feathers metallic and soft. The click-whir-clank of mechanical contrivances, the hiss of steam fills her ears and overflows, overloads her. The glass tinkles and tangles in front of her eyes. The bird brings her to the first tooth, sweeping down, down, down.

Time is rushing past Child, a stream of color and sound, of the words of trees and the grumbling of the earth. She is in the time before, when the Mothers were young, were just putting on their faces, dipping their fingers in the sea to wash their gritty eyes, dabbing the white silt on their eyes and the red clay on their lips. Fire blooms across the hills, devours mountains and rains ash upon them. A white glow creeps from the west, devouring everything in its wake. Slim white shards loom against the sky, flying titans seeking shelter from whatever holocaust they unleashed upon their own world.

Child sees Razor-Teeth combing her hair with the ribs of a whale, tying mammoth bones and strings of colored boulders into the wild, long strands. The first Children huddle at her feet, praying to her for safety, though they are as but ants before an elephant.

And then there is Knife-Fingers, tall and hungry. Sharpening her fingernails on the Pinnacles, she leaves the deep rifts known only as the Claws to Child's people. She hunts those strange, flying ships that fought their way from the blinding horizon to drop their loads of death upon the land, spearing them on her fingers and devouring them whole, while their helpless weapons slide from her skin. It is her cruel hands that push back the light while Razor-Teeth and Fire-Skin rear fences that tower into the impossible. Eons pass, the Children become great and beautiful as the Mothers age, and it is the Children now who build the fence ever higher, reinforcing it, fending off the predators from beyond.

Ships crumble and break against those fences, and their bones become mortar in the watchtowers. Fire crackles against the towers, but Fire-Skin licks it from the walls and spews it back against the attackers.

"There," shouts Child. "Follow her!"

The bird sweeps downward. The heat of the young earth slaps across Child's face, suffocating her.

Knife-Fingers stalks away from her Sisters, and the chase begins.

Child sees the fragments of a thousand unrelated lives, flashing by, trying to snatch her from the hunt. Knife-Fingers does not wish to be followed or found. She alone did not leave Children to guard the new world, and she has fought her battles. And yet…Knife-Fingers shapes and changes things everywhere she goes, molding mountains and hills, creating lakes where she steps in the mud. Slowly, following the Mother, Child learns to narrow her focus, to see only that which travels full-circle to influence or affect Knife-Fingers. Free of the myriad distractions, time doubles and folds on itself, hurtling them through a swirling world. They speed through history, the images impacting themselves in Child's memory, new events spinning out in front of her. A new war erupts, the Sky-Father unleashing his rage and greed against the Mothers, seeking to layer the earth in water so that he may see only his own face. Child watches as the Mothers seduce the towering Lord of the Skies and lay him low, wounded and pleading for mercy. She waits for his death as Knife-Fingers rides him, but he breathes on, long after the Mothers leave him.

Now, Knife-Fingers bears Children, and they are unlike the others. The elder Children have become lazy and slow like their Mothers, but these new Children were born of war. They look upon the desolation of the earth and desire for it to be made whole. They lack the terrible might of their elder cousins, the ability to change their forms as they will, but they are mighty, made of stone and steel.

They set their will upon the world, and it is remade. At long last, the light is pushed back from their borders. Heroes hunt down the things that have grown in the land, bringing back tooth and tale to win the notice of their Kings. Peace spreads across the world, and the Mothers subside as the third age of their Children comes to its fullness.

And yet…there is rot within. The Sky-Father's body is dead, but his restless soul is trapped within. Tormented, forgotten, bitter beyond telling, he poisons the land and calls the last evils to him…

With breath-stealing suddenness, the world falls away from Child, and bitter cold sets into her bones. Someone snatches the eyepiece off of her head and dumps her on Razor-Teeth's tongue again.

"What has happened?" she asks, rolling onto her belly. Sudden nausea rolls through her and she vomits burning bile.

"You were trying to look into the future, child." The librarian crouches over her. He dribbles ice-cold water into her mouth and drapes a blanket over her shoulders. "That is not my place to show you, and the bird ceases to work if he is taken too far. You might have been stranded."

Child shivers and shakes, disoriented. "How long has it been?"

The librarian stands. "Long enough for you to become thin," he said, "but not so long that you died. Winter has fallen."

Child groans and struggles to sit up.

"Lie down and sleep until your soul catches up to you," says the librarian. "Your steed is well-fed, and winter must pass before you may set out again."

Even the shock of the lost time was not enough to keep Child awake.

Child takes many more rides on the bird after she wakes. Each time, she follows a trail, a path through history. The early Kings, the other Mothers, the Queens, the Children. She follows the spider web of their influences, explores the strata of their experiences, but she finds no answers, no clues on the answer that she can take to the King. She still does not know what her quest is, what she is seeking, what she will bring back.

She reaches back into the past and finds Wildfire. She stalks the flaming Queen through the many years in which she cowers in the caves while the world drowns around her, watches her eventual return to the sun to dance. By this time, Child not only watches and listens, but feels, too. The songs are in her blood, her head, her soul.

So she dances in Wildfire's skin, the same joy and wonder flooding her veins, a silent passenger. She is gone in this thread for a long time, consumed with curiosity and desire.

So, winter slowly passes, spring approaches. Though snow still clings to the shoulders and head of the Mother-Mountain, Child speaks of leaving.

Loath to lose the company that he has enjoyed so much, the librarian begs her to stay.

"I am on a quest," says Child. "I shall return, if I live."

The librarian smiles, his wrinkled face shifting into a sly, knowing grin. "You have already died," he says. "But you will never return here."

"I *will* return," she says, and kisses him on the cheek before she departs.

"Be careful," is all that he says. "The path you choose to follow is seldom the right one."

The fire-horse has found a narrow valley where grass grew thickly enough and small shrubs provide him with plenty of fodder. Child finds him by the trail of charred skin and ash.

A short, plummeting, heart-stopping flight back down to the plains, and the steed takes his original form again.

Child turns him north, and they are off.

The teeth said that Knife-Fingers hides somewhere to the far west, half in the sea and half on land.

She leans forward and speaks in the beast's ear. "Find the Western Sea," she says, "the Breasts of the All-Mother."

A snort, a tossed head, and he is off.

The western shores are said to be an intangible, impermanent thing, stretching the width of the world. Bloody-Eyes sits in the depths at the Heart of the Sea, her shifting and snoring sending waves miles inland sometimes, where she floods the coastal plains.

But, intangible and vast though they might be, they are also very far away. Child grows tired of the journey in short order. The Ramble-Shack Mountains, through which the steed is taking her, are filled with wide holdings. She spends many of her nights in the halls of these lords, regaling them with tales of her adventures with Wildfire and Mother-Mountain, her quest to find the supine form of Knife-Fingers. Her legend grows, and her name begins to take shape, whether she wills it or no.

The courts are beautiful or grim, well-appointed or dusty with age, and all terribly, terribly alike. The peasants go about their tasks in the deep clefts of the valleys. Burly horses haul plows through the stony ground; fat ponies clop their way to market. Children herd geese and sheep bleat on the slopes.

It frightens Child a little, to see such peace and calm. The Children of Chaos are not loved by order, so it is with a glad heart that she comes down again to the edges of the Walking Sea.

The fire-beast draws to a halt, snorting. The treacherous ground here shifts restlessly. Sharp shells poke up here and there, volcanic debris and the detritus of a hundred ruined ships. In the distance, the masts of a great war-ship jut against the horizon. The sea roars in the distance, creeping towards them.

The steed does not want to continue. "Change and we will fly," she says, stroking his neck. "You will not drown."

So he again begins that horrible rending of flesh and bone. Living fire bites the ground where his blood drips down his twisting forelegs. Again his clawed wings throw a wide shadow, but he settles onto his rear legs and steps forward, gingerly.

At first, his movement throws her around, violently, for he is low to the ground and runs like a clumsy man on crab's legs. Eventually, she grows used to it and does not question his decision to remain on the ground.

The Walking Sea has left puddles the size of small ponds, many of them teeming with life. Child can see brightly-colored crabs and hissing sea-snakes, a tiny squid strangling a fish to death. Small packs of scavengers pause to watch them pass. The beasts—the size of a small dog—are sea-plump, finned and gilled, but with webbed feet and hands and eyes that look at her all too shrewdly. They sift constantly through the sand, their hands plucking shells, wood, bone, and glass from the sand. The steed passes close by one such pack, the watery sun catching on the strings of bright shells and glass around the creature's necks.

Child cranes her head to watch them. The pack leaves its scavenging and begins trailing them. "Faster," she whispers to her mount, and he speeds up as well as he can.

Miles pass with the pack in their shadow. Child fingers her sword, wondering if she can fight all of them off if they decide to attack. They come across an old sea-buck, foraging in the kelp-bushes. The pack splits off and gallops after him. Child's stomach heaves at the sound of the scavengers' laughter when they catch the old beast. She cannot not resist looking over her shoulder.

Pieces of the buck litter the sand, ragged edges and shreds, and two pups play with the smashed head.

Child is glad to leave the flats and travel into the low hills beside the sea plains. Here, houses tower on sturdy stilts, ladders leading to the silty ground. Gardens flourish on high platforms. The singing of the women in the garden carries pleasantly to Child's ears.

She guides her mount out of sight behind a hill, and he becomes his first shape again.

The villagers are kind to her, starving for news of the outside world. They are an isolated people and ply her with food and drink while she tells them of her adventures. They draw a map for her of the Walking Sea and tell her where the Mother might lie, and how to get there, but insist that she spend the night with them. It is not safe to travel at night through the hills, they say.

Child, glad for a bed after so long on the road, does not argue.

The next morning, she sets out with a full pack of dried fish, hard bread, salty cheese, and other road-worthy food. A seal-skin map hangs from her belt. Singing a merry song, she guides her mount through the hills, not thinking of the echoes that come back, twisted and whispering vile things.

Though the sun burns bright and hot in the sky above, it is as if light falls on either side of the hills through which she travels. Tendrils of light stab the boundaries and shades to be swallowed whole and hidden by slowly-moving shadow.

The fire-beast is nervous, keeping to the center of the road. Child dismisses his fear, attributing it to the proximity of the sea. But he shifts under her, his horns spiraling and branching out of his head, plates of bony armor sliding over his haunches, chest, and belly. His claws sharpen, dagger-wide teeth jut over his jaw. He shifts and warps and changes into a dozen shapes until she is angry with him, but still he is uneasy.

Deeper they travel the path leading downwards and sideways and through hills and valleys. Child is quite lost and bewildered. She had been told that the other side was a mere three hours' ride, but the path leads on without sight of an end, and night is quickly shutting out the sun whole.

The path twists, doubling back on itself, crossing underneath the previous track. It branches in one direction, and then another. Child draws her sword and the steed speeds into a trot.

Darkness falls quickly as they descend yet another ramp in the trail, into a valley of sheer cliffs. Down, down, down they go, the narrow eye of daylight above them fading. Stars glimmer in the sky. Fog closes the path, obscuring the ground and the sky.

Child's heart rattles, ragged and loud in the all-consuming mist. Even the steed's fiery coat is now drowning and muted. With a terrible, heart-stopping terror, Child realizes that they are still in the sea-hills and that the high tide might drown them like vermin on the floor of this featureless, nameless valley. The horse falters, side-stepping nervously on the road.

She leans down and clutches his sparse mane in her chilled fingertips. "Don't stop, don't stop!" she pleads. "Forward! Forward or we will die!"

Her voice echoes off of the cliffs, rebounds. Horrific laughs, desperate pleas, mangled cries assault her ears, her own voice, but not. "Forward, Courage," she says, naming him, and lays her forehead against his mane. "Forward and we will see the sun again."

It is not for her promises that he suddenly leaps forward. Ears plastered against his skull, he gallops down the stony path, charging toward whatever waits for them.

Child raises her sword and tightens her hand in the mount's mane. She screams a war-cry, and they meet the Hounds of the Sea in the depths of the chasm.

Dark beasts they are, glowing with the phosphorescence of a recent feeding. Dog-like bodies, their legs and paws lined with suckers like some terrible underwater monster, they stand half the height of her steed. Some of them cling to the walls of the chasm, which by this point is narrow enough that she can touch it on either side, if she spreads her arms. It leaves her little room to swing her sword, and she bleeds from their whipping claws within moments.

The steed screams, swinging his great horns and slashing at the beasts with his claws. Catching one hound in his jaws, he batters it against the cliff and flings its limp body into the mass of its pack.

Water falls on them from above. Child risks a glance upwards, although she takes a tentacle to the face for her efforts.

The tide is rising.

Courage bellows his own challenge and pulls himself into a new shape.

Four long arms, legs tipped with the clawed feet, a head filled with nothing but sharp teeth, he flings himself up the wall. Clinging, scrambling, biting at the hounds that come too near, he climbs out of the cleft. Water spills over the opposite wall. A thin stream runs down the to the valley floor. The Hounds cluster around them, above them, beneath them, still snarling.

"Forward," begs Child, and Courage scrabbles sideways down the thin ledge.

The water rises and the creatures of fire tremble in terror when it surges and licks at their feet, their path not so much above the floor of the valley.

The Hounds are all around them, nipping off flesh and yipping when it burns their mouths. Many of them swim in the rising water, their shapes becoming as long and smooth as sharks, flitting through the water with ease.

There is no ramp, no gentle exit from that end of the valley. Only a sheer ending, and had Courage not changed, they would be trapped. She turns and looks over her shoulder, seeing the masts of tall, red boats bearing down on the mouth of the valley. The mist of a falling sea cloaks their decks, but it seems to Child that living bodies are tied to the masts.

They reach the top of the cliffs as the sea fills the valleys and claims all foolish enough to live near the shore.

She turns her mount as they reached the great rift. Indeed, bodies do hang from the masts and the sails, and are fastened to the outside of the hull, living mastheads. The helmsman, lashed to his wheel, steers them straight into the rift, and the two red ships teeter for a moment on the edge before the sea pulls its singing tribute into the depths.

She wheels Courage and they flee the Valley of the Sacrifices, the first to escape, perhaps, in centuries, for the houses of the Sea Kings are built with human bones, and their drowned horses haul chariots made of ship wood.

At last, following the footprints of the Walking Sea, they find Knife-Fingers. They have had to fly much of this path. Knife-Fingers is restless, as though she dreams of the future, and the shoreline has become inconsistent. The sea is a churning, filthy, stinking thing here, yellow with piss.

The decaying Mother looms on the horizon, an indistinct lump covered with sea-creatures. Seals bark and wallow in her out-flung hands, forgetting their danger, for the Mother wakes infrequently, but is ravenous when she does.

Encrusted with slime, pockmarked with parasites and bleeding, infected wounds, the stench catches Child from some distance. As they wing closer, she wraps a scrap of shirt around her mouth and nose. Even Courage wrinkles his nostrils and snorts repeatedly.

Birds nest between the Mother's toes, staining her soles with shit. Dirt and sand are mounded up along her sides. They come to her at low tide, and a vast reach of red-stained sand spreads around her crumpled form. As Razor-Teeth was vast and awesome in her stony silence, so Knife-Fingers is terrible in her stinking, disgusting torture.

Child dismounts some distance from the Mother and leads Courage around the mounds of dirt and debris.

She has found the Mother. She looks around and wants to weep, to laugh, to feel joy, but there is nothing. Faced with the end of her task, she is empty. The birthmother of the God's Sons lies before her, a treasure greater than the Pearls of the Phoenix.

Suddenly, she is aware of another loyalty, another task. It had lain in the words of Fire-Skin, in the touches of Wildfire. They have sought the Mother for millennia. Only Child has found her. She owes the Fire-Children many things. She loves Wildfire.

But this stinking, rotting thing is no danger. The wounds left by Fire-Skin so long ago still smolder, sinking, slowly, through her skin, hissing when water drips from some crag of skin above. A hand is nearly severed, the fingers still touching some of the boulders strewn across the sand.

She draws near the Mother's hip. A bony, rough surface, pitted with dead clams, with more wounds where birds and beasts have fed on her.

She does not know how to wake the Mother.

She climbs back on Courage and directs him into the air. Child rides him over the Mother's face, galloping across her eyelids. Finally, she dismounts and beats, screaming, against the Mother's cheeks.

She has failed.

Desperate, she remembers a story, a story in which mortals drank blood from Bloody-Eyes' veins and became mighty heroes and where maidens suckled at Razor-Teeth's breast and became seers, witches.

The story of the birth of the God-Kings, one cast down by them for fear that mortals would seek to rise so high.

It is her only hope. Child empties her water canisters and draws Wolf Tooth. Weeping, sick with disgust and guilt, she hacks at Knife-Fingers' flesh, at the nearly-severed arm. Perhaps the Mother will not feel it. Perhaps it is no longer necessary. When, finally, blood gushes out, it is dark, slippery. But the same blood wells around the Mother's eyes, and Child knows it is all she will find. She fills a canister with blood, gagging at the stench.

She climbs onto Courage again and flies him to the Mother's breast, where milk still leaks from her pitted nipples.

She has done it. Her return journey is nothing more than a haze. The courts cheer as Great Beard, grimacing, drank three swallows of the blood, the Queen two. Their sons each painted their tongues with the blood. They were whole, vital, God's Sons once again. The rest of the blood has been given to the sorcerers. Great Beard will not grow old so long as the blood remains. Meanwhile, the sorcerers will study it, perhaps unlock its secrets.

Great Beard and Silver Tongue's gratitude has been great. Gold and jewels, horses, the hand of the Princess. Everything Child could desire. So why does she sit here, on the cliffs overlooking the sea, far to the south of the tower? Why does she weep?

Her thoughts are a tangle. She has succeeded, but she has nowhere to go, now. She dares not return to Wildfire. Guilt will not let her report the Mother's place to Fire-Skin. She can smell the smoke, knows they are hunting for her.

Why does the Court not see? The taint is spreading through the sea. The black, greasy tendrils of rotten blood riding the waves, searching the rivers. The Mother has awakened. Her blood calls to her. But the child is different now. Rotted, old, corrupt.

Child scrubs at her hands again. The smooth surface is tainted, slippery with blood. She has dipped her hands in fire, in wine, in everything she can find. Scrubbed them with horsehair, wire, sand, even the edge of her knife.

And the King had wanted to honor her with a name. Is he so foolish? Tie a rope to her soul, a rope that the Mother can follow? She feels it now, the seeking of the Mother. It wants her. She is a child of Fire; she has stolen blood. She drank the blood of a Mother, she, a no-name hero.

They are hunting her. They are all hunting her and she is caught between Fire and Sea.

Now she understands why the heroes have vanished, the rumors of curses on their lines. She understands it and rues the day she answered that call.

She leans over and vomits, but only black, greasy blood comes up, and smolders in the dry grass.

As My Daughters Were to Me

SEVEN TO ONE. *One to five. Five to three. Three to nine.* Sticks clatter in patterns, picked up, laid down, spinning through the air with an acerbic whine.

Above as below. Below as between. Between as within. Within as without. Invisible words, heavy with life, mortality, meaning.

A woman steps into the world. Black water flows with her, pooling around her feet, wrapping up her legs to clothe her, rolling over her shoulders like oil. Strangler-hands dangle at the ends of her arms, fingers slithering eagerly against each other, tipped with jagged long claws. She stands silent and waits for her sisters.

Below as between. Between as within. Within as without.

The sticks clatter again. Bloody red light explodes from the center. As loud as her dark sister is silent, the new demon roars from the light. She is naked but for the skins of dead things and sheens of blood, fresh and drying. Long yellow teeth jut from her upper jaw, curving over her chin. She howls a hunting-song.

Within as without. Without as between. Between as above.

Gold. Silver. White. Light without form. The sticks clatter and something shatters, breaking sound and light to shards. Music from somewhere beyond. Voices spun through crystal and honey and razor-blades. She is there, wavering and flowing as a mirage at sunset. Pale and perfect, glowing with her own inner light, shimmering with an alien song.

She stares silently, joy and terror consuming her equally. She has summoned the Three, a feat none have managed before.

It will cost her life. She knows this. She could have snatched a sacrifice, some hapless slave from the streets, but then Slave would have manifested as well, and she is not useful to her plans. She wishes only the strong half of the Wheel, the ones born of betrayal and loss.

The gods of Clay and Chain do not bind her; the goddesses of Star and Stone do not see her. She is beyond them, and now she has done what even they cannot.

They come to her, their empty eyes dripping promise.

What would you have from us, pure one?

"My people are dying. We have lived so long as slaves that we do not understand how to fight. They take our children and women, break our spines, and bow our knees until we beg them for more. Our power lives only in our blood, and our masters spill it into their cups to give them visions."

Dark fingers touch her back, the rough cloth melting to rot. Soothing cold numbs the welts of old beatings. She hides her hands, too late, and her blood mingles with the wild one.

"They bleed us dry in our pens so that they may have a moment of dream! We don't dare to destroy ourselves. We can't bear to live. We cannot flee."

Is that not the lot of the mortals?

"It should not be," she roars, and feels her lungs tear. "If our gods must desert us, why can we not be masters of our own destiny?"

You do not wish to be. You were, once. You created the gods. You named them. You shoved yourselves into their loins to be born as slaves. Do you think that they wanted you?

"Then why can we not be rid of them?" She is dying. Her hands no longer have strength, withered as sticks. Her legs crack, the bones trembling to dust.

You are too weak. They try to make you strong, but they are of your own creation and your dreams were very small.

"Then teach us to be strong! Let my people rise. Give them back the voices your sons stole, and let them call Star and Stone!" Her fading voice turns crafty. "Or do you wish to be the slaves of Clay and Chain forever? Have you grown to love their soft pricks and rough ways so much?"

Laughter ripples, funeral bells and war trumpets.

You give us so much credit, and so little. We are not gods, and we do not know where your voices have gone.

"Liars," she whispers, and sinks her broken fingers into the pale one's arm. "Bring back the glory of my people, and I will name my death-gift to your freedom when the task is done, but let them sing again."

We have been away too long, I see, your kind have forgotten how to fight their own battles. Very well. We grant your wish. Regret this, and remember us.

The pale one pulls forth her blood, which beads in the cold of her hands, forming six great red gems that glow with their own cruel light and seem to laugh. Each sister sets one beneath her tongue and falls upon the dying summoner, rending what they need from the ruins. A crown of finger bones, set with staring eyes and another jewel. A cloak of flesh, fastened with lips holding another jewel in the torn tongue, and a strangler's rope of hair and sinew, weighted with the last jewel.

They take that which they desire and leave in a swirl of dark water, washing into the hills on the shoulders of the looming storm.

They are not there when a fourth figure rises from the red mud of the pit that birthed them. Shrouded in soft darkness, she kneels next to the torn form of the summoner and lays gentle hands on the broken face.

Oh child, what have you done? she whispers, covering the wreckage with her cloak.

The voice, slurred and broken, is not spoken so much as felt. "Mother told me stories of the old witches, who could call beings to life. I did not think it could be done. I do not regret it."

The dark one holds her peace, smiling benevolently at the summoner. *In the old days, your body would have been found and shrined to watch over the village 'til your soul was pleased with its deeds. You would have been worshiped.*

"There is no one left to worship me."

No, but if your will is great enough, I may have a task for you that my daughters cannot do themselves.

"I will do anything you ask."

Then live, and follow them. You will know when your time has come, and as they are my daughters, you are theirs. Do not falter when the time comes.

The summoner stands, grey as the storm above, hard as resolve and soft as hope. She stares in wonder at her hands, whole and strong again, feels her face. Her fingers falter when they come to her mouth, tongue-less.

A quiet sound of amusement makes her turn to face her savior. *How do you think my daughters were born?*

Her speech was taken, but she remembers the trade-sign of the plains. *And how were you born?*

The dark face turns cold for a moment. *It is not your concern. You are of the Stone-godlings now, and you will know your mission. Be gone.*

The godling flees, stumbles as she discovers the beginnings of her power, and vanishes in the direction her mothers have gone.

Lightning crackles over the bare hilltop, though an observer might have seen the shadow of a tall woman and her horse for the briefest moment, but who can say? The hills are full of secrets and memories.

Dreams of War

IT WAS THE WARS, she said. The short-lived fools of other worlds built bigger weapons, more vicious poisons, competing with each other to have the deadliest assault, until they buried the universe in fire. That was when the white light started, when the moon burned white and the stars disappeared beneath their hungry younger sibling.

The great ones were consumed in that fire, she said, standing athwart the world and buying us time to build our walls and shelters. They held it at bay for a time, their flesh burning from their bones until only their skeletons held watch. The magic even in their bones was so great that the fire still recoiled from them.

Their children held the next line, as we built underground gardens and museums, storing the wealth of our world deep in the earth. Our people, who love most the stars and the night winds, retreated within earthen walls in a bid to survive the death unleashed by those who did not even know the name of our kind.

The Roar of Red Silk Banners

THEY SAY SHE COMES forth only under the darkest moon, or on storm-ridden nights when there is no chance of light.

They say her face is white as milk, networked with the scars of her magic.

They say she is always silent.

They say she can make the dead sing.

They say she is the daughter of gods, or the mother, or the jailor.

They say the Nameless One and the Blood Drinker are her sisters, or daughters.

They say many things, the people of the plains and the people of the mountain valleys.

Many of the things they say are right, but none are true.

The moons are dark tonight, only the faintest sliver of the Shadow looming low on the horizon. The Dark Month, when no rain falls and the winds from the desert are wicked and leaden with sand, the day is only a few hours long and colder than the dark sea murmuring endlessly at the edge of the salt-grass steppes. Winter is looming. The tribes have retreated to their strongholds, and the citadels nervously check their stores and walls.

Utter silence rules the narrow canyons cutting across the steppe; even predators are silent on such a night. Gods move quietly through the waves, keeping their own council.

The whisper of red silk banners is nearly lost under the whine of the midnight wind, the thud of muffled hooves nothing more than the beat of a fearful heart. The Hes Ut tribe sleeps soundly, secure in the ancestral pact that war is suspended during the Dark Month.

It is their death, but it is quick and unremarked. A small tribe, religious offshoots of their ancestors' faith, they hold the Council of Queens to be heresy, and so there is no one to miss their presence.

The red silk banners whisper back into the night and are unremarked, for none are left alive, and no sign of their camp is left. Only the blood in the soil can tell tale of their demise.

I remember the day she found me, the day she reached out her hand and caught the lost fragment of my being, the day she put me beneath her tongue.

I might have killed her—I feared for a while that I had—for all the wisdom and knowledge that piece could hold filled her with light, incandescent with power and loss. But she was already on the threshold of her own great death, already fighting to hold on. Perhaps I might have been the last straw, the last blow she needed to fall, but no.

She hears that there are many who believe her possessed, who believe that a foul thing took refuge in her black heart and uses her to its own ends. I know the truth: there is not a being in all the voices of this universe that could use her to its own ends. No, I came within reach of a creature unready to die, and she used my power to become a power of her own.

She is glorious, this daughter/sister/champion. Her gifts are not ones that I would ever have thought fair, nor kind, but she is just beyond all reproach, and kind enough, in her dark way. There are no wrong-doers safe from her eye, nor fell demons that do not quail at her name. She has her reasons, and her laws, and they do not bring her love or admiration, but the rightness of them brings her comfort.

She. Oh, how I long for them to see her as I do. For them to know the agony that the sight of another's suffering brings her. She. Blood-drenched and wrathful, her neck ringed with the sacral bones of those she has visited justice upon, wracked with agony over those she has not protected.

They paint her a killer, a murderess who drinks blood and revels in destruction. They tell tales of a grim red beast stalking battlefields and beer halls. The men terrify each other with stories of wife-beaters and child-killers being torn to pieces. The women whisper of a demon who will avenge them if all else has failed, a woman bearing the same scars they do, a creature who feasts on kings and peasants alike (though the truth is that she will bring vengeance for any wronged creature, woman or beast or child or man, regardless of form or sex).

She. The murals do not show her tears, do not understand that we weep over each life lost. They would show justice as a child in white, blameless and innocent. They do not show the scars on her back, the bruises that mottle her chest and belly to this day. They show only the ragged scar around her neck, that fatal wound that gave her the sight to claim my power and kill her greedy, foul master.

She sits now, silent, her red horse silent beneath her, and watches the war. It is a little war, as these things go, a war started over a woman who chose to escape one brutal master for one who might be less brutal. It is a war that will not make very much difference, not as we see things, but it matters to those inside the walls, to those waiting at home.

Night is falling. The soldiers are withdrawing, returning to their camps to sleep. The defenders are seeing to their wounded, repairing what walls they can, clutching their children close. If the tables were turned, they would bay for blood, but they are, for tonight, in fear. It is not the women and children and soldiers who choose these things, but the kings.

It is twilight, and fog slithers from the restless sea to cloak the city and camp. Our horse's hooves are silent in the red mud and mist, its nostrils flaring in displeasure at the stink of offal and death. White shades mill restlessly as they rise from the mud, blood dripping steadily from their death-wounds, her presence calling them forth earlier than they would normally rise. She is the end of the war, and they may return to their homes in peace.

The camp is loud with laughter and the relief of having survived another day. A few screams draw brief silences, but the city is about to fall. They are nearly home, and wild with anticipation of plunder and ruin.

They do not see her. They rely on their scouts and their dogs, but she does not wish the scouts to see her yet, and the dogs slink to her heels, silent and obedient. The horses recognize her, and proud warhorses drop their heads and round their backs, begging to be left alone.

There is no warning, only a mist that turns red and clings wetly to their legs, and then she is there.

Even I am curious, for she has never faced an army before. I ready myself, in case I need to lend my power, but she dismisses me, comfortable in her own strength.

I had not realized how greatly she had become, how ferociously she had accumulated force.

Renowned warriors cower or fall to their knees as she enters the camp, a wave of silence spreading before her. She is not a physically-imposing woman, but on her red horse, her skirts dripping blood, the quiet click-click-click of the bones she wears, the contained fury she radiates…this is enough. She does not need my power to cow them.

Not a word is spoken as she progresses through camp. The horses break their tethers and follow, milling with the dogs in a silent parade. The mist thickens until it is as though blood is pooling around their ankles. The stink of fear intensifies; it is only a matter of time until one snaps, challenges her—

There.

He is not particularly big, but his body is covered with scars, and the shadow of a berserker spirit rides him. He squalls with terrified fury and races for her; his voice should shatter the silence, but it is muted and only deepens the fear of the others.

She waits.

He is nearly on her before she raises her hand. Against a berserker, she is no match in hand-to-hand combat; against a spirit, she has no challenge. She closes her fist and he crumbles, red-hot ash pouring from his nose and mouth and ears as the spirit dies, wailing. She is not finished, her fist clenching again, and he doubles in agony. It is now blood pouring from him, and in moments, he is dead at her feet.

She resumes her progression. Twice more she is challenged, twice more, her answer is silent and swift.

On the other side of camp, nearest the city, she halts her red horse and reins her around. Still, she speaks no words but watches the camp for a moment before simply…disappearing from their sight, though we can still see them.

The silence holds for a moment, before utter panic takes its place. The animals, loosed from their fear, bay and scream and panic, fleeing in all directions. The men, the men are not so wise, and huddle together, waiting for morning, their priests praying loudly the night long, for they can all feel our eyes on them.

Their night is long, but they are so close to victory, and in the morning light, they tell themselves that it was all a dream, that the tithe of dead men found in camp fell victim to unseen wounds, or sabotage, or the cold damp. They will not abandon the war so easily, and turn to the city walls…but they set foot within weapon-reach of the city and the earth turns to red sucking mud, pulling the first of them down before they understand what is happening.

Time and again they try, and many more are lost. See? She is merciful, but humans do not like to admit their fear or weakness, and many more died than she wished.

And then she reveals us, just for a moment, insubstantial as smoke under the grey skies, and finally, it is enough. With shouts and cries of terror, they flee, all order and dreams of glory abandoned, their ghosts behind them.

The city watches in bewilderment, suspecting a trap. They will not sleep comfortably for many nights, but they have seen her, too, and the red hoof prints of her mare from where we revealed ourselves will show for many more years than the youngest child will live.

She. I did not know what she would become that day, when she seized me and placed me under her tongue, when she took divinity in her hands and turned it to her own ends. She is young still and only beginning to find the barest glimmerings of what she is.

My death ruined all the great things that I built, destroyed the peace and beauty I spent myself on, but if she is the greatest of the things that have come from my death, it was not in vain.

All the World is Made of Ghosts

I COME TO MY senses in a field of bones, of scavengers, of red mud.

I am not alone.

Around me, brothers and enemies are lowering their weapons. Rifles and machine guns splash into the puddles at our feet, broken bayonets glinting dull in the strange light. A fog has lifted, and we stare at each other, bemused, forgetting why we fought.

Around us is only silence—a deep, ghostly silence. Bird and beast have fled, the echoes of mortars fading. The armies have marched to a new front or fallen back to a desperate encampment.

I do not know or care. I know only that I have fought my war.

My feet itch and ache. Mother always said that the farm's dirt was in our very bones, that we could never go so far that it would not call us home. Now it calls, a tether pulling me east.

Dirt in my bones, my boots, and my lungs.

I do not remember the way—where are we, anyways? I have only ever marched where they told me to. I did not bother with maps.

The dust remembers.

I look for the wounded, to save those that I can, but there are no corpses on this battlefield, only rain-bleached skeletons. It is us, the bleached dead. Crows still haunt the field, looking perhaps for shreds of flesh, but there are no wounded here to save from their beaks. Perhaps the wounded were taken away while we fought. I cannot remember much. I only remember home.

Snow falls, wrapping the bones in its cold embrace, melting on the steaming red mud. Now it is only us, and we have lingered too long.

I turn from the red field. Into the forest. My brothers beside me, in red and green and black, men of many ranks and armies. The bars and patches weighs us down, iron crosses and screaming eagles, sickles and stars, the emblems of a war that left us behind. Our war is over; we are going home. We did not care what brand they wore before, and we do not care now. Our war is over. The bright insignia sinks into the red mud, and a weight lifts from my shoulders.

The black fingers of winter-bare aspen trees clutch at my sleeves. Their white trunks loom through the mist like crooked bones against a grey sky. White and black cattle in grey fields. Grey men pouring red blood into black mud. We cannot stop the bleeding of our wounds—from heads and hearts, guts and joints, it flows down our bodies to stain our feet, a red path to our last battlefield.

Yet we do not weaken, so soon we ignore it and walk.

We walk, endlessly. We have no watches, no radios, no bugle calls or sergeants bellowing *Fall in!* We have no time, and so we walk, retracing the steps we took toward the Front. Shedding our hatreds, our fears, our uniforms, a trail of history discarded with the honor it deserves. Red footsteps pattern the white snow.

Instinct guides us away from towns, from settlements. We remember too well what we did to those quiet places, the destruction we left behind. We did not want to.

We were hungry, driven, lost.

We had orders.

We were shot if we disobeyed.

I cannot remember why I did not stand firm. Evil is so very clear in hindsight, and so very excusable in heat.

I was young when I left, in search of glory. No more than a farm boy, thinking of nothing but kissing girls and how long it was until dinner. Big and raw-boned, awkward in the dances.

There were a lot of dances, when the officers came. A lot of pretty girls hanging on my arm and kissing me for good luck while they spoke of glory and honor, of the great victories we would surely win. The officers spoke very convincingly of how we would save our homelands and return as heroes, and many of us signed (these were the days when we could sign, before the uniforms were put on us by force).

They put a gun in my hands and pointed toward The Front and said, "March!" When we stopped, they fed us and maybe they taught us to shoot, or they ordered us to sack a village where our aunts and cousins and sweethearts had grown up. Those were the good days. The bad days are being swallowed by red mud and grey dust.

Now the only food we need is the thought of home and family. Everything else tastes of dust and rot, even the bright red apples—they hang withered but our childhood memories say they are oh-so-sweet—in orchards gone wild in the genocide of their caretakers.

We walk, and the dust in our bones calls us home.

After a while, the thoughts stop. After a while, there is only a will, a hand hurting with thorns but unable to resist. After a while, there is only the grey road under my feet and the endless gnaw of cold and hunger, a gnawing that sets into my bones and does not leave.

The road under my feet is grey. My footprints are red.

We split into smaller and smaller groups. Soon we are few enough that I see faces I know.

Wilhelm, the farmer.

Pjotr, the butcher's assistant.

Markos, the horse-breeder (and he is the most fortunate, for three of his beloved horses have come with him, their hoof prints white in the dust, where ours are red). We walk in silence, wrapped in the dust and the thought of home.

The forest no longer clings to us, its arms weighted with snow. The crows still watch and wait for us to fall. The sky is still grey, though surely we have been walking for months. There is no time here.

Grey shades pass us from time to time, in old trucks or wagons, on foot or on horseback. Their forms waver in the wind. They do not hear our tentative greetings. I suppose it is not surprising that the ghosts we left do not wish to speak to us.

I wonder, sometimes, where the people have gone. Did we kill so many? I do not remember. I remember a constellation of yellow stars passing us one day. I remember a village set ablaze. I remember…

I do not remember. The grey dust closes over me again, like my mother's arms protecting me from my father's wrath.

The roads are empty and the world is made of ghosts.

This is our village. Grey stone houses and barns of weathered wood. Thin black and white cattle in grey fields. White horses, tails tucked against the bitter wind. Ragged trees bearing withered apples.

We are home.

We dash apart, calling the names of our loved ones.

Nana! Mama! Anna! My father is dead; my brothers died under the tanks before we were subsumed.

Marja! Elena! My mother, my grandmother, my sisters, my sweetheart. I call each of them, my heart ablaze with joy.

My cries echo hollowly between the buildings. In the distance, I can hear Wilhelm and the others crying, too, but only the crows answer, and the distant lowing of the cattle, as though through fog.

Anna! Marja! The horses and cattle live; there must be someone here. Chickens peck at the ground near the door of the house. Maybe they are all inside. Maybe it is breakfast time.

I have found them, and my heart stops. They are thin and colorless, like the shades we saw on the roads. Their bright shawls are as grey as their skin. Black hair and black eyes, staring fixedly into nothing. They move around each other, passing plates at the table, going through the motions of life. As though through a fog, I can hear their voices, subdued and grieving.

Why do they grieve? I am the one who has come back to a world of ghosts. I left so that they would be safe, and here they are, dead and mourning.

Mama! I am here! Elena! Marja! But they do not hear me. I am too late.

The others tell the same story, and when we stop, wrapping our fingers around the faces of our loved ones, we see that they are old and worn. Our hands slip through their forms, though sometimes one will pause, and shiver, as though they have felt something from afar.

So here we are. The village is empty, though a few other men return in time. We have reached an understanding with the ghosts. They make the motions of work, and we follow behind, pounding fence posts and feeding stock. We are not hungry, but we take pleasure in the sight of the memories of food and home. If we listen carefully, we can hear their stories, hear them reminisce about us, about the days before war.

And the trees are white and black against a grey sky. The cows are white and black in grey fields, and our red footprints linger still in the grey dust of the endless road.

All the world is made of ghosts, but the dust in our bones brought us home, and our war is over.

The Tears of Some Lonely God

GOLD FLAKES, fine as ash, fell around her feet, catching in her dark hair like the tears of some lonely god.

The apocalypse was…brighter…than she'd expected, limned with temple-gold and the poisonous green of a dead sea. Before her, a supernova of fire and debris blooms, shot with vivid red and orange, the glory of the sun at its heart. Trees crumbled around her, instant carcasses in the blast wave. Splinters combed her hair; cinders bit holes in her silken garments.

She had stood at the heart of many conflicts—the trenches of the Great Wars, the walls of Troy, surrounded by Mongolian hordes, the hills of Gettysburg—the toils of gods, kings, and heroes. War was her lust, the blood of nations her wine, the prayers of the dying her lullaby.

She was birthed for this, and yet this moment frightens her in a way that nothing else has.

She had waited so long for this, Kali the Mother, the Eater, the First One, wanting to see the end. Her hands had shaped this world, guided its strange people along their bloody path. She had given them the atom, fission, and then she had dabbled her fingers in a few wombs to create monsters: hungry, hopeless things who couldn't paint on any canvas smaller than the halls of history.

Her children had learned well. Watching the cloud, she wondered if she had gone too far. Given them too much, led them too long. They loved this darkness, the taste of death on a cool night's breeze, the cries of motherless children. They had made war of art and art of war. They did not want an end. They chose an eternity, an endless night of annihilation.

Below her, the lights of civilization choked. Halogen-lit skyscrapers, lovers' candles, lantern-lit huts. Another cloud rose, scattering the first column, sucking noise and light into its hollow cheeks and spitting the ruins out in a ruined tide of debris.

In its wake came the firestorm, foundry flames drawn into the vortex and vomited forth, tearing through the last bits of the city. It drowned her in a torrent of malice, slapping aside the rich, bitter taste of a good death.

There was no good death here.

None.

Only the sludge of a crushed civilization, salty and flat.

A third cloud rose and a city of nearly a billion people disappeared without a trace into the dust, their bones glazed into a glass desert.

She trembled in fear of what she had wrought. The bones of murdered mountains kissed her cheeks, and she drew her wings around her, turning from the carnage to seek refuge.

If I Am Your Slave, Oh Lord

THE DRILL BREACHES AGE-STIFFENED membrane, *chews through the thickening veins. The lines in sector seven have backed up. The ground swells, threatening to spew rotten blood across the city. What a terrible loss of power that would be. It could cripple half the city for weeks.*

The siphons suck away the crystallized pus, dropping it into collection bins. Glowing softly with radiation and fading holy power, the chunks are the rarest element on the dead Earth. They power the city.

Another crisis averted, another sector of the Dead City saved. It is only one of a thousand such crises. The foundations of the city are rotting and their resources are drying up.

But they battle on, uncaring that as they wheel gaily through the wreckage of time, their holy beast stumbles and weeps with agony.

He is old and rotten. Time caught up with him long ago. Abandoned by his lord, his people, Azazel is sloughing away. His body is riddled with human maggots, the descendants of those he saved from the wrath of God. He stumbles, staggers, spreads his wings to keep balance. The bridge embedded in his thigh catches on the Dover Cliffs and sends him hurtling forward. They crumble under his momentum, bone and stone. To fall would be to kill them all. To keep walking is to die. To keep them alive is to die. He can't shake them off, he won't shake them off.

They are his: his children, his masters. All he has left.

His vengeance.

He shrugs his shoulders, shakes his head side to side as though his mane can still whip away the blood-sucking flies. His hair has long since been harvested for building the cities; it is strung through him like an aerialist's web, holding the cities to his innards. Thick as a man's thigh and tougher than spider-silk, this is the thread of heaven. It is still strong enough to stand the wrenching. His intestines rip instead, spilling the waste of a metropolis in a stinking stream down his legs.

The pain eases, the vein is tapped.

The infection is bleeding off, fueling the great, roaring machines of the ancient city, the sick-green glow of waste-lamps lights the streets in the eternal night. They have learned to be frugal. He is all they have, and he is nearly eaten away. The last angel. The last city. The last humans. Wandering on a dead Earth.

They've excavated his belly. The stark silver of inhuman bones shines in dull radioactive shimmer, an arching cavern under a thin shell of back-flesh. Drying intestines coil in his pelvis, unsupported by any other organs. He is an angel, what need does he have of innards? The intestines were only left to be hoses, pipes for waste and fuel for the humans, but they are wearing out, and there is nothing to replace them.

Already the human parasites have built a colony in his sternum, hanging their houses from his ribs, setting hooks in the little flesh that remains. Sky-scrapers rise from his hunched back, anchored in vertebrae. Needle-thin reactors jut from his thighs.

If the city had a song, it would be organic. Slip, squish, squelch. Its heartbeat would be the irregular staccato of the machines. Nothing like the endless slippery streets, the houses dripping blood. The sickly-sweet scent of composting flesh where strange plants grow to supplement the quickly-disappearing meat of the angel. These are the things they have grown accustomed to, and now all there is, the only life left on this forsaken world. So time passes, and things move on, and there is no outside world. Only the swaying, stumbling universe they have carved out of Heaven's cast-off.

Sometimes his disease overcomes him and his flesh rips.

Just a few minutes ago, a house tumbled—flaming—into Azazel's hips. He feels the embers now, scorching flesh. If he could speak, he would tell the parasites to come and feast.

Come now! It's cooked! It's clean! Come and eat me.

Sustain yourselves, we're all dying, he wants to shout. Come and feast while you can, while your endless clocks tick-tick-tick and tock-tock-tock, telling a time that's gone.

He is old.

The first angel, the first beast, the Angel of Death, Lucifer's dark twin, God's first disappointing son.

He was there at the beginning: nameless, with trembling hands and body as slight as a whisper. He was there at the end: his blades singing and his dark cloak heavy with soul-stain and memories. It is the end he remembers because the beginning was too long ago. He remembers all the things of the dead and so his own memories fade away.

But he remembers the end, oh so well!

His steed, Famine—tall, swift and thin as refugee child—devours the living things of the earth: bodies and grass and trees and beasts. Famine's breath scorches the green things, and his hooves churn the endless bodies into the black mud as he follows after War's armies.

Azazel opens his mouth, sorting the souls of the damned on his tongue, tasting their fear and their hatred. The holy, he is not permitted to touch. Gabriel has already snatched them away, burned their earthly bodies with his holy flames and strengthened his armor with their purity.

Azazel strides through the remnants of the greatest cities of a dying Earth, the expanding sun shining from the edge of his guilt-sharp scythe. No soul is spared his wrath.

It takes seven years for them all to fall, for the wicked to be burned up. Seven years of killing, of glorying in his holy task. Seven bloody years in his service of the Lord.

And, when it is over, he stands astride the corpse of the planet. The ashes of the wicked rise to his mighty knees. He raises his weapons to the heavens.

THE AGE OF EVIL HAS PASSED! he cries. *Let the fires of the Lord burn this planet clean, let foulness wither and pass!*

The storms ride at his shoulders, the lightning flickering blue and yellow on his blades. The glimmer of deepest night is in the depths of his executioner's hood.

IT IS FINISHED, he cries, and the echo of his mighty voice shakes the Earth itself. The wail of lost souls sounds from the blades, from his hands, from his hood, the stained that cannot not pass into the Devil's bloated belly.

IT IS FINISHED. Let the wicked be cast into the deeps. Let me return to your arms! He cries to the sky, begging for an answer, to be allowed home. He remembers, faintly, the comforting flames. He remembers the certainty of love in Gabriel's eyes. He has served his purpose, and he wants to go home.

Gabriel looks down and laughs at the Reaper, at Azazel's torment, at his longing. He is the Lord's best love, now, though his blade drips with blood, and his mouth is blistered by cleansing fires.

You shall never return here! The golden face of Gabriel, wreathed with flame, twists into terrible glee. *We are finished with you, tainted one. You have served your purpose, served it and we are done, done with you forever! You are alone, soulless one, alone in the darkness with your beloved sinners, with your steed and your cursed blades. Death and Famine and War have no place in our new Earth. Begone, beast, and join your brother in his pit!*

On and on, Gabriel mocks him, and no matter how much Azazel calls to the Lord, only the bright countenance of the Archangel answers him.

The Angel of Death falls to his knees, roaring his agony to the cloaked stars. The fires of his son, War, burn around him, but the warrior had fallen in the end, consumed by his own weapons. Famine withers, bereft of life to claim.

Azazel is truly alone. He feels the poisonous air seeping into his veins, tastes the ashes of the charnel house born on the endless winds.

The corpses of his sons litter the landscape. His brother is chained, doomed to wander, the Damned captive in his belly and throat and dragging at his feet and his proud head. Lucifer has no hate left to give.

Azazel fingers his broken blade and ponders his self, his abandonment. There is nothing to live for, surely. He *is* Death. His power is all-reaching. When the stars end, when the world crumbles, he will be there. Not even the Lord has been able to keep anything from his grasp; those the Lord has claimed have been delivered through Azazel's hand.

With a roar of fury, he drives his hand down on his sword and screeches, not from the pain, but as his flesh knits itself back together around the blade. Screaming in all the tongues of Earth, he hacks at his hand, his legs, his torso and head and back and thighs.

Die! he roars, chopping himself into bits, into messes, the flesh knitting as fast as he could cut it. *I WILL DIE!*

I am the master of all! I will not be forbidden my reward! If there is no place for me, I will DIE! His great wings beating the bone-ash into a billowing cloud, he rises from the ground and flings one dark sword into the sky with all the power of his ancient flesh. *And if you will betray my devotion, then I shall betray your trust!*

There is no answer. His sword falls back to the Earth some time later, the blade rusty and seared by the acid sky. He leaves it there, jutting from the ground, and staggers on until he falls again.

51

He lies in the ashes, heaving with the pain of his loss. The river of his tears mixes with cinders, burns his eyes blind. He beats his hands against the ground, the flat of his palms tearing on the skeletons of long-ago buildings, the Babels of the modern Earth. He drives his hands down on them, tears them through his hands, stains them with his blood and claims them as his own. He rips the jagged core of a skyscraper out of the ground and gouges it into his heart with a squelch.

The flesh knits around it, absorbing it into his body. A momentary calm descends on him. It is still here.

The world has not vanished. The endless darkness still holds shape.

He staggers to his feet. His brother is somewhere, perhaps deep within the ocean by now, or high in the shattered Himalayas. Perhaps he has answers. With each step, his flesh tears on debris. Stooping, he drags his fingers through the refuse, catching up bits of this and that, a scavenger, a collector of rubbish, a broken angel knitting his heart together with memories and destruction.

He walks through land and sea, through the darkness and the radioactive wastes and the hellish glow of the dying sun, but he does not find his brother.

But, somewhere in the sea, on some deserted speck of an island, he finds hope.

His stinking, ravaged body forges the burning waves, his fingers automatically sifting, straining, searching for something to remember the past. And suddenly, there, in the middle of nowhere, he catches up a tiny island, a tiny island with the unmistakable heartbeat of humans.

Somehow, here on the dark side of the Earth, in the middle of an ocean as hot and rancid as a pot of burned sewage, they have survived.

He cannot not speak, not to them. He can sense their fear, their hopelessness, and he holds his hand out to them.

Come, he wills them, *come and make a home in my heart. Come and find refuge, and we will survive together, we will disprove His power. Come, please!*

And they come, the poor and dying, mad with the end of the world, and he places them in his chest.

I will be your meat, and your oil, your god and your home, your refuge until the sun dies and we are all that is left. I will guard you until He comes to destroy what remains, and we will show Him that he has failed to impose himself on everything.

We are sin. We are Death. We are free.

So they build a city in his flesh, forged from the scraps of civilization embedded in his body. They marry and bear children, and their children marry and bear children, and Azazel strides across the Earth, keeping them from the burning sun, standing strong against the storms. They burrow into his flesh to escape the ravages of weather, hollow him out, and he is glad for it. They are all that is left to him. They are his weapons now.

Time passes, the Earth's spin slows, gravity weakens.

His flesh does not protect them when the sun explodes, and thousands of them die, burned to ash. But he crouches on the dark side of the Earth and wraps his wings and arms around them, and some live.

They have colonized his wings by now, dredging roads through the scarred, seared flesh. His skull is hollowed out, rebuilt to catch the constant rain, which is then pumped into his veins to separate filth from water.

A mighty civilization, fed on the flesh of the greatest angel, raised on tales of the Lord's vengeance, has been born. So he staggers through broken time and crumbling earth, bearing his people on his back, and humanity is born and fucks and dies and evolves and survives.

They are greedy now. As humans will, they have grown numerous. His reserves are draining. Never fat, what little there is has been harvested and refined for food and warmth. His flesh, they have eaten or built homes from. He is a shell.

His movement is disrupting their cities. Buildings fall, too ramshackle to withstand his staggering steps. So they send an expedition. His tendons cut, Azazel falls one last time to his mighty knees, and knows he is betrayed.

It is an eternity that he is locked there, and the humans finally realize their mistake. He is all that stood between them and their final death. He shielded them from the elements, from the storms. Without his movement, they are the prey of these storms.

Thousands of them die, though Azazel wraps his wings around them again. It does not matter if he dies.

It is their life that saves him.

He is fading.

Lucifer stands in front of him. His face, once as beautiful as Azazel had been terrible, is marked with the lines of agony and eternity.

He is returning, says Azazel. *And I am too weak to fight Him.*

Lucifer kneels by his brother's side, takes the great head onto his shoulder. He strokes the mess of the fallen angel's face, weeps over him.

I will be here. I will end him, I and my damned children. But I can't save you.

So be it. With his last power, Azazel comes to his feet and sends his spirit through the blood in his veins, through the great machines running ceaselessly on his back.

The civilizations on his wings, in his chest, cry out in terror, and are consumed. As he had once fed them, now he feeds on them. He devours their essence, births them as new angels, terrible and fell and mad.

Take what is left, he says to Lucifer.

Lucifer's head drops back and he roars. Souls sweep from his lungs, his belly and his mouth. He, too, is hollow, worn away by the malice of the survivors.

Feed on him, he says, and they obey.

And as the light of Eternal Dawn spreads across a landscape that should have been dead and defeated, the sons of Azazel seize their father's weapons and turn their faces to the hosts of the Lord. In the moment of the Lord's victory, as all worlds watch, war is joined in the heavens.

Dreams...Elsewhere

THERE ARE MANY WORLDS, my great-grandmother once told me, many more worlds than we have names for. Some are populated with strange creatures who speak and build cities as we do. Others are barren, or echo with the voices of lost civilizations. Each, she claims, must have their own place in the Dream. She wondered many times if they still survive, if there are any far enough, or with great enough heroes.

Some of their stories came to us, brought back by our explorers or snagged from the skies, passed down through the ages, learned in dreams.

She told me few of these stories, but she wrote them down. Grand storyteller that she was, she could never bear to let a single tale die.

I turn brittle pages and trace the Broken God's dreams through the lives of other worlds.

First Step, Last Breath

HORUS CLASS 7 ROSE above the gravel field, slowly filling the banks of windows. Massive, black, it blotted out the smaller islands behind it.

The ship banked slowly, rocking as the small asteroids bounced off of her iron-clad sides and ran through the net tunnels to shower harmlessly around the ship.

"Drop anchor over the center of the island," said Moset. "We don't have long until the rock moves out of the Aether."

The navigator nodded, turning the wheel. Engines belched and men scrambled through the rigging. A tiny asteroid, barely the size of a pea, pinged off of a sailor's helmet, having slipped through the nets. The man cursed, the sound carrying down into the control room.

"The Aether is different here," remarked the alchemist. "I've never seen it so purposeful."

"We are in the thickest reaches of the band," said Moset, "but so near the dark edge, the Aether becomes strange and unpredictable."

"Sir, storm approaching!" cried the lookout, his voice echoing through the voice-horn.

"TAKE COVER!" cried Moset, throwing open the hatch. Out here, in the "beaches," the belts of gravel and sand caused by the erosion of larger islands, a storm could be particularly deadly. The nets siphoned off larger rocks that might cause damage, and the iron exoskeleton surrounding the ship knocked away the rocks too large to be held by nets. But a storm so close to the island, where gravity was so unpredictable and the rocks so small, could easily scuttle the ship.

The storms did not touch me on the island. For that, I could be grateful. A piece of the ship hangs just outside the gravity of the island. The storms have torn it apart, the wood and iron floating in shreds.

Men poured through the hatches, diving to the floor and tripping over each other in their haste to get out of the way.

Moset slammed the hatch down, seconds before the storm hit them.

Aether storms could be as small as a ship or massive enough to span the entire belt. Completely electrical, one would often start in the extreme reaches of the Aether, near Helios, and set off chain reactions through the band, until they swiped out at the other end, far worse than they had started.

"How big is it?" asked Herakleios, the first mate.

"Not as big as the last one," said the navigator. "Won't be able to touch down for a while though."

Moset sighed. "Alright, get some sleep and food. Be ready to respond immediately."

The men stampeded to the living quarters, and Moset took a seat against the wall. Strapping himself in, he peered through the window at the approaching storm.

"I think we have discovered why the island hasn't been explored before," said Helios. "I've never seen this much activity in the Aether."

"The Eye of Horus," said Moset. "The storm belt. I've touched the edges of it, back when we were hunting the Apophis Eagle."

The men fell silent, watching the gravel bounce from their windows and sides. The storm was short-lived enough, and Moset rang the bell, signaling everyone above-decks again. The men scrambled, hand-over-hand, into the rigging, and the navigator brought them over the island.

Gears snarled as the massive anchor dropped. The landing crew shimmied down the chains and wedged the anchor's prongs into the heavy boulders. The ship lowered ponderously to the island, hovering close enough for the rocks to scrape her sides.

Moset unstrapped himself and stepped above-decks. The gravity, heavier than Earth, made the walking hard for men who had become used to the weightlessness of the Aether. He stood at the railing in the semi-darkness and looked out across the bare rocks. No plant-life here.

But the food, the water, that did touch me. There is nothing here. Nothing but foul insects and slugs. It shames me to admit it, but I did eat them, once. They made me mad, seeing things in my vision that were not there, dreaming of beautiful music and the colors never found in the Aether.

The giant gangplank dropped, and Moset stepped onto it after a moment of hesitation.

Step one. Step one onto a new island. Step one onto a new hope. Step one into the rest of life? Moset hoped so. White rock, black dust, green sky. A severe beginning for a hope.

It was all Moset had, though, and so severe would have to be enough. At the end of his leash politically, his contributions to Kimet all made during the last Pharaoh's reign, Moset needed a victory.

The darkness is closing on me, rapidly now. The Aether thins, my vision blurs. Oh, gods of my people, why have you done this to me?

He needed a new ship, too. That was his real worry, as he stepped onto the unnamed island, Horus Class 7. The journey here had been...unique. Veteran of dozens of Aether-journeys, Moset had never been through so many storms or ridden such a rough course. Fairly sure that an Aether-ship shouldn't be bucking like an ill-tempered donkey, Moset had to consider that there really might be something wrong with her. So many memories haunted the ship.

They had found the Apophis Eagle, brought him and his mate back to Kimet. The Pharaohs used the raptor's offspring for war. Mere mention of the bird brought hushed voices and fear.

Things lurk, out here. A sea of half-dreamed monstrosities, as though I am under the sea and the salt clogs my eyes. Rippling shapes in the constant half-night. Gleaming teeth flashing near the pit I hide in. I ventured out once, you know. Looked around to see if anything had died on the rocks. I found bones. Bones bigger than my thighs. They had been gnawed on. So had the rock around it. The tooth-marks, some of them were bigger than my fingers.

They had completed a mapping expedition, hauling priests, astronomers, cartographers and flunkies from one end of the Aether to the other. Of course, a month after they returned from that, some sort of quake shook the Aether and it all changed. His maps were obsolete and considered semi-collectible curiosities. Yet, it was something no one else had ever done, then, or now.

He'd never named his ship. She was just "she," or "lovely," or "good girl." He'd never married. He didn't need to, not with the Aether waiting to be explored.

My monster isn't the only one out here. Terrible things haunt the Eye of Horus.

Now she was aging. Deep gauges scraped her sides where a storm had caught them unawares and dashed them against the Horus-Ledge. The fine carvings and gilt on her bow wore smooth under the ceaseless chafing of ropes. The nets spread around her body had more patches than net.

She had seen better days. So had he. They were both old, both relics of the golden age of exploration.

He patted her and led his team onto the island. The navigator tossed down a coil of rope, and they all tied themselves together. That was a lesson he'd learned on a previous mission. The Aether made things deceiving.

Lords of the Air, does your gaze not turn to the Aether? Is it outside of your realm? Does it blind you? What plague have you sent on us? What have I done to deserve your wrath?

Sword in hand, Moset glanced back at the ship one last time and led the way through the jumbled rocks.

Their sandals slipped and slid on the greasy stone. An acrid stench filled his nostrils, a reek of fire and sulfur. As they progressed towards the center of the island, the stench became stronger, and they saw tiny fires burning in crevices and craters.

"This rock is evil," said Ankhmahor.

"What burns though?" asked Moset. "And why? What would start a fire here?"

The men drew nearer to each other, glanced nervously around.

The fires still burn. They must have been set as a warning. But were they set by the guards, or by the exiles? I never heard of a prison-ship coming home.

"Let's go back," said Moset. "The island is not so large; we shall explore it once it is unshadowed by Ares."

Quick as rats, the men scampered back to the camp, nearly dragging Moset with him. He sighed, wishing his seasoned sailors back with him. This lot had been scraped out of taverns, prisons, off of whores, and forcibly marshaled onto the ship. Only Moset, Herakleios, the slave Shadouf, and the navigator had ever been into the Aether before.

Moset untied his rope and contemplated retiring to a village somewhere. Preferably somewhere without Bast, the ship's dog. Bast, the overly-demanding dog who was currently sitting on Moset's feet and howling.

"Cat-like indeed," muttered Moset. "Even the cats are quieter than she is."

"She missed you, sir," said Herakleios, grinning. "Why didn't you tell me you'd married her?"

They'd discovered her outside of one of Bast's shrines, in some backwater village. Sleeping in the meager shelter of the shrine, eating the offerings, the hound certainly seemed to have the blessing of the cat-goddess. Her name was not mocking, but honorable. However, Moset did sometimes wish her name was more common so that he could use it as profanity.

Moset sighed, shoved Bast off his feet, got bitten on the ankle for his efforts, and hurried into his quarters.

Bast sat outside the door and howled, pathetically.

"Mother of the Nile," muttered Moset. He grabbed a chunk of hard bread, leftover from his earlier meal, and lobbed it out the door. The howling stopped.

The crew unloaded the ship slowly, setting up a camp in the little valley they had anchored in. Bast ran around camp, howling her occasional comment on the place, and upsetting any piled gear she could find. She found some scent and chased it around camp, over rocks and between men's legs, until Shadouf grabbed her and tied her to a stake. Nursing the bite he'd received for his efforts, Shadouf ignored her whimpering and set up his tent around her.

Moset watched as the crew erected the common tent. His own quarters would be to the side of that tent, where he could keep an eye on the gear. The navigator would pull up the anchors and move out of range. Less chance of mutiny.

The sailors were getting better food here than they did on the ground, so Moset couldn't see why they would mutiny. Then again, why did slaves revolt, knowing it was doomed? He shrugged and spread a sheet of papyrus on the table.

Once the common tent was erected, Moset set up his blankets inside and changed into clean clothes. Water, at a premium in the Aether anyways, appeared to be non-existent here. Their stores would have to be carefully spread among the men.

I have to retreat, again. The size of the island saved me for a while. Moving so very slowly through the Aether, the front edge slipped from breathable air while I was sleeping. That alone, those brief moments, was hell.

Bast's howling brought him running out of the tent, half naked. Several men followed as he scrambled up the piles of rocks, following her voice.

The little black hound cowered at the bottom of a deep pit, a natural scar in the rocks. Fires burned around the outside, oil oozing down the sides of the pit. The rope Shadouf had used to tie her lay next to her, bitten through.

"Go get the ropes!" he yelled. Two men ran back to camp.

Moset stretched out on the rock, feeling the fire scorching his side, and talked soothingly to Bast. When the men returned with the rope, he tied it around Waset's waist and lowered the boy slowly into the pit. Bast whimpered, her leg crumpled underneath her.

Waset gathered the dog into his arms and started to come back to the edge. "There's another hole here!" he yelled. "Like a tunnel!"

Bast whimpered again when the boy bent to peer into the tunnel.

"Bring her up here," said Moset, "and we'll look at the tunnel after we've explored the top."

They pulled Waset up, the boy cradling the whimpering hound against his chest.

Shadouf splinted Bast's leg, and she took over Moset's bed without asking. The one thing the men all agreed on was the dog's welfare, and so he grudgingly slept beside her, wide-awake and listening for sound, any sound. Even the men's loud snores were diluted in the Aether.

Moset finally drifted to sleep, but it was thin and rough, as though his senses still trained on the things around him.

Exploration of the island took only a few short days. Heartened somehow by the lack of life on the rock, they turned their study to the burning liquid. Slickly black and unctuous like tar, it did not burn when exposed to normal fire. But, when exposed to the white fire burning on the island already, it sprang into flame so quickly that one man was badly injured.

Bast healed quickly and began hobbling around camp during the day. She never again set foot outside after dark, or went near the pit.

After the island was explored, and the alchemist was sufficiently supplied with the ingredients to study the oil, Moset put together a small search team. Waset, small and limber, went first, armed only with a razor-sharp knife. Moset followed, sword in hand and bags of food and water at his belt. Some of the men carried rope, and Ankhmahor followed Waset, carrying a torch. Ten men let themselves down into the pit. Shadouf came last, his broad-bladed desert sword strapped across his back, a long knife in his hand.

Ankhmahor doused his torch in the dripping oil and lit it from one of the fires. The light flared more brightly than ten torches, and they slid through the first hole in the rock.

The first room, barely large enough for all of them to fit into, took Moset's breath away. Used to the massive spaces of Kimet and of the open sky, he felt the rock pressing in on him. His chest tight, he looked around, and saw the same fear on the faces of all of his men. Bai doubled over and retched. The scent of vomit filled the air.

There! There it is! Do you see? A flicker of deeper darkness. A glint of something metallic. Don't you see that? It is all around me, darkness and glitter.
And, it is gone.
Back into the tunnels.

"This place is cursed," whispered Bai, holding his stomach. He looked at Moset, appealingly. "It's cursed. We shouldn't be here!"
"Nonsense. We will go on." Moset struggled to draw breath into his lungs. Buried alive. Buried. Tons of rock above and beneath him. Endless space around them. Panic threatened, again, and he shoved Waset forward, finding comfort in movement.

It has become as dark and stifling here as it was in the tunnels. Without water, I have tried drinking the oil. It slakes my thirst not at all, but it seems to keep me alive. Why do I wish to be alive? If I starve, I will not feel my breath being stolen away, one bit at a time.

Waset led the way forward, down a narrow tunnel. Forced to hunch over, curses echoed off the walls as men knocked their heads or elbows against the stone walls, or tripped over the rough floor.

Fortunately, the oil did not seem to trickle so deeply, and they were in no danger from their torch.

When the tunnel ended and another small room opened around them, the men clustered around Moset. He nodded encouragingly and took a small drink from his water-skin. The floor of the chamber was coated with a thick, fine dust. Every movement raised choking clouds of it.

Bai marked the way they had come with a splash of white paint, visible even in the shadows. Shadouf knelt and ran his fingers through the dust. "It is pale, like the ground bones my people's enemies use to paint their faces."

The men laughed. "Then do not tell them about this place!" said Ankhmahor. "They will all come here and dig up the stone for dust!"

Shadouf looked at them in disgust, but was silent.

The desert people speak of wild demons, djinn, creatures haunting the wastes to destroy mankind. They speak of the beauty and awfulness of their demons and offer sacrifices to them. Perhaps this is where the djinn came from, or perhaps it is where they go when banished from Earth.

The path branched here, and they took the left path. Waset and Ankhmahor stayed a little in front of the others. The path deepened, tall and narrow now. The light of the torch seemed to diminish here, failing to illuminate the shadows. The dust rose in great clouds, no matter how carefully they stepped. Arms scraping either side of the passageway, they stopped and tore strips from their kilts, wet them, and placed them over their mouths and noses.

With this protection, they followed path after path, searching for some sense in the direction of the tunnels.

"AIIEEE!"

Moset whipped around, scraping flesh off of his arms. "What is happening?" he yelled, straining to see over the other men.

"Bai has fallen!" said Shadouf, running back along the passageway. The tall slave knelt next to the smaller man. Unable to pass any of his men to get to Bai, Moset could only rely on Shadouf.

"Is his leg broken?"

Shadouf stood, slowly, and turned back towards the men. He held up his hands, glistening wetly. Red. Blood.

"He has been cut open," said Shadouf. "His guts lie in the sand."

Waset keened, his eyes wide with fear. "What beast has done this?"

Shadouf bent down again, and Moset wished he could see over the men. The slave held up a massive shard of some sort, coated with blood.

"I do not know what this is," he said slowly, and handed it to Djoser, who passed it down the line to Moset.

He took the shard and beckoned Ankhmahor to hold the torch close. The shard was rock, black but veined with a greasy resin. A bit of it stained Moset's fingers, dark as old blood.

"We will keep this," he said, "and have the alchemist run his tests on it."

"We must go back!" said Djoser. "I'll not die in these tunnels!"

"Do you want to go back, alone and in the dark?" asked Shadouf, his voice low. "This thing, whatever it is, is behind us. We keep an eye clear, and we move forward, and maybe we survive."

"You just say that because you would see us all killed, SLAVE!" shouted Djoser, shoving the tall Libyan.

"Enough!" shouted Moset. "Shadouf has been through many dangers with me, he fears nothing. But, should you wish to go back, Djoser, I am sure the danger will miss you."

The sailor snarled but said nothing more, and they continued on their way.

Once, Shadouf shouted, and as Moset turned, the slave's knife shot sparks from the wall. Something hissed down the tunnel, fleeing.

Shadouf screamed a war-cry after the creature and raised his sword in victory. Black blood dripped from the blade, red blood from Shadouf's chest where claws had raked his shoulder, barely missing his neck.

Moset nodded. "We will take the upwards tunnels and hope that it leads to the surface."

Ankhmahor lit another torch from the old one, and they moved on.

They took tunnel after tunnel, each branching one way, and the another, until they would have been hopelessly lost, had not Djoser been given Bai's paint, what little was left.

Always, they could feel the beast behind them. Shadouf kept his sword in his hand and moved sideways through the tunnels.

Another room opened in front of them, and they circled around Moset.

The screech drove them more tightly into the circle. Something drove at them, all teeth and claws and blinding wings. Shadouf leapt at it, screaming his war-cry, and drove it back again.

Bloody scratches ran down the slave's side and legs. Ankhmahor lay in a pool of his own blood, his arm nearly torn from his body. Shadouf knelt next to the man, searching the wounds with his fingers. Ankhmahor gasped for air, inhaling the dust of the cavern. Already, mud caked his wound.

Shadouf looked up, shaking his head. Moset nodded, and Shadouf quietly drove his knife through the base of the man's skull.

No one said anything as they set out again. It was time to survive, not fight. The dust grew thicker, their footsteps silent in it.

Alone on a rock, lost to all living thought, it seems even the gods do not hear or see me. It leaves much time for reflection. The tunnels are behind me. Aether collects, pooled, in the chambers, and so I might survive there, for a while. But the mystery still lingers, the dread of an invisible death that took each of my fellow men and devoured them at the edge of our sight. Their gnawed bones, I flung from the edges of the island. There were ten of us, one Turn ago. Now? Now I am alone. Alone except for the beast that haunts the edges of my sight.

Moset's mood darkened as they walked. He did not know what they were searching for. They had only entered the tunnels to find some source of the oils above, or perhaps, of the flames. Shadouf was wounded, Bai and Ankhmahor dead. The beast was still out there.

Weight settled on his shoulders. The shadows closed around him.

His feet dragged in the dirt. With everything in his body, he wanted to turn, to run back to Kimet and retire to the countryside. He didn't have the guts for this anymore. He was old, old and frail, and his thread would soon be cut from the tapestry. With sudden desperation, he prayed that he would not die here and be left to rot.

The room opened around them, almost unnoticed. The ceiling furled up, the top of the camber widening. Shadouf raised his torch, and the others did look then. They looked up, into the flickering shadows, and every man saw a beast crouched in every one of those shadows, waiting to drop. They looked ahead, into the widening space, and felt the beast waiting for them.

Nearly paralyzed by fear, they inched forward. The air was cool here. As their eyes acclimated to distance again, they looked up and realized that stars shone in the rifts of the ceiling above them.

Muted cheering. They knew where they were now; those very vents had puzzled them from the top. Indeed, there was one of the torches they had dropped, hoping to see the bottom!

Moset knelt to pick it up, his fingers sinking into the dust. Something hard and cold met his fingers. He curled them around the object and pulled a slender bone free. Human.

"Mother Isis!" exclaimed Waset.

Moset forced his fingers to uncurl, dropped the bone back into the dirt. "Men have been here," he said.

"And died here," said Shadouf. He knelt beside Moset and ran his fingers through the dust. Teeth, bone fragments, finger-bones caught in his hands, and he lifted a handful. Dust trailed from his grip, fine and filling the air until they choked.

"I've heard rumors," said Shadouf, "that in the old days, the Pharaohs abandoned their worst criminals on some remote island. This started not long after they gained Aether technology. During the Great Plague, they filled every ship they had with the victims and sent them to the same place they sent the criminals."

"Hades," said Herakleios, the sole Athenian member of the party. "Our senate has done the same thing. Anyone with plague or considered irreversibly evil, is sent to Hades to die."

Moset let the bones trickle from his fingers, swallowing hard. "How closely guarded is this secret?"

Shadouf shrugged. "I only heard it from a whore who had been servicing a captain. He'd talked too much, and she shared willingly."

Herakleios heard the meaning. "The concept is not too secret, but the location..." His voice trailed off, and he examined his ragged nails.

"The location?" prompted Waset, panic in his voice.

"We signed our own death warrants, coming here."

They were all silent for a few moments.

"There's plague in every inch of this rock," said Shadouf. "And if anyone survives, they would be desperate and inhuman."

"Like the beast attacking us."

Shadouf nodded. "Who knows what the Aether does to men who do not die?"

There, again! I see it, I see the madness coming for me. There is no face. Is there anything more horrible than that? Who do we turn away from in the street? The man without a leg, or the man whose face was burned away in fire?

This creature was not burned in any fire. Its face is simply a blank mask of scars.

Moset closed his eyes. "It passes from the Aether for a while, they must die."

"These caverns are endless," said Shadouf. "Who is to say that they have not found a way to preserve life?"

"We must get out of here, at once!" Moset rose to his feet, his face grim. "OUT!"

They searched for hours, but there was no exit from the chamber that did not lead farther down into the labyrinth.

"We must go back," said Shadouf. "The beast has most likely not entered the cavern. I will take point."

No one argued with the slave. Moset followed Shadouf, and Herakleios took the rear, armed with two swords.

The beast did not attack them in the endless hours. They felt it, glimpsed flashes of eyes and teeth now and again, but it did not come to them.

When, finally, they rose to the surface again, the fires burned more brightly than ever, and stars filled the sky.

A great light lit the horizon; they were approaching the edge of the Aether. Crossing the rise to their ship, the smell of smoke hung in the air.

And, as they turned the last corner, ready to sob with relief, they stopped and sank to their knees.

The ship burned. Stripped of everything useful, and burned.

They ran among the wreckage, searching for bodies, for possessions. No bodies. Only smears of blood, shreds of flesh, a hand here or there.

Everything was gone.

The beast crouched in the wreckage, one look at them, leapt away faster than they could follow.

A chunk of the ship groaned and slipped from the edge of the island, falling towards empty space.

The island was on the cusp of the Aether.

Their ship was gone. Their food, scattered. Their supplies, destroyed.

A quiet whimper, and Bast slunk from the wreckage, her sides burned. Her ears, ragged with tears and blood, perked as Herakleios knelt for her, and she ran to him, crying.

Shadouf slumped, his sword clattering against the stone. Waset sobbed. The other men huddled together and turned angry eyes on Moset.

He had gone too far. He'd pushed too hard. Greed had brought him here, and pride.

"Forgive me," he whispered, horrified.

"There is no forgiveness," said Herakleios. "No gods will hear us here, except the darkest, and they should be kept blind."

Moset bowed his head. When he looked up again, the men had left, withdrawing towards the center of the island. Away from the pit. Shadouf and Herakleios, still bearing their weapons, stood aside and gazed towards the pit. Their soft voices did not carry to him.

Moset was alone. And, alone, he cursed the gods and his own pride.

The edge of the Aether draws near. Below me, the beast lurks in its caverns. How it survives without air, I do not want to know. Shadouf and Herakleios have gone to hunt it. Bast went with them, brave little thing. But I, crippled in my ka, *cannot raise a hand to feed myself. I lie here, soiled, ashamed, broken.*

Is this the end of my story? To die here, without blessing, without coin or preservation? I will not travel to the Afterlife. I will be caught here, haunting this barren rock, this cursed prison. The criminals, the plague-ridden vermin, my only company.

Oh, Lords of the Air, what did I do to displease you? Where did your mercy go? I brought you the Apophis Eagle and his mate, I brought you maps and ore, glory and honor. I gave you my life, I gave you everything there was. There are no children to carry on my name, no wife to mourn me. Even my ship, shattered on a nameless rock.

It is here again. He is faceless, that beast. Maybe my worst fears gave him face. Perhaps Apophis, angered by my stealing the eagle, has sent vengeance on me. Who knows where this thing came from? It is evil. It is here to kill me.

I am here to die.

Shadouf, I hope you have found some haven. You can survive here, if the beast can live. You can avenge me, my old friend, and someday, bear my body back to the temples.

It fills my sight now, fangs and foul breath on my face.

Lords of the Air, hear my prayer. Deliver me from the Void whence I am doomed, deliv—

The Shadow of Phrixos

THE POETS OF ATHENS speak of the slow dance between the Moirai, the goddesses who decide the life and death of all men. Clotho, Lachesis, Atropos, spinning, measuring, cutting the threads of mortality. Each of us has an allotted string, a span of years we may live.

The poets of the lower air sing the praises of the lords of fair winds, cry prayers to the gods of the storms and the sun. Their songs are full of joy and bold life.

The poets of the Aether whisper of Sigaon, Lady of Silence, and of Phrixos, Lord of Silent Fear. Sigaon throwing her dark, musty cloak, ragged with the thrashings of noise and disorder, across the Aether. Hushing it.

Phrixos, daring to kiss the cold Lady in the deepest reaches of the night that never ends. Together, they hold men silent. Captive to the fear of their own voices, of attracting the attention, the anger, of Phrixos. Terrified of tearing a new hole in Sigaon's cloak.

She weeps, they say, when that cloak is torn. It is the only clothing she owns, and if it is too torn to wear, she will be naked and forced to accept the gown offered by Phrixos. And if she dons that gown, he will take her to his bed, and she will be his wife, and supreme goddess of the outer Aether no more.

Only those in the deeps the Aether know Sigaon's name. Her name has never been spoken on earth, there is no silence deep enough to call her. Phrixos stays where he may watch her, lurking out in the darkness somewhere, beyond the Aether.

None of us wish to lose the patronage of the Lady of Silence. None of us wish her tears, nor want the care of Phrixos. We love our goddess for her tears, her gentle care. We do not bear any love for Phrixos.

We are foolish men, but we are not that foolish yet.

I am Sophronios. I keep watch over the farthest reaches of the Aether. My home is the rock Gnathos, also called the Jaw of Phrixos, the coldest and most distant from Earth. The lad Aegidios is my only companion. When I wake, he sleeps, and when I sleep, he wakes, and so we keep unceasing vigilance over this tiny piece of the Aether.

Unceasing vigilance. Unceasing silence.

Our only task is to watch the colony Haliartos. The colony, mining some rare ore, (men such as us are not told what this ore is, nor do we ask!), hovers nearly as close to the edge of inhabitable space as Gnathos. The priests pardoned us of our crimes to watch this place and report all things which might happen. We make sure that no ships come to the colony, except the holy triremes. Beyond that, I am not sure what we are to watch for. No one but the priests knows that we are here.

There has been nothing to report for eleven years. Every year, the priests visit us, bringing the necessities of life and leaving with the wealth of Haliartos.

Eleven years of silence, of contemplation and devotion to Sigaon. Every day, the tiny offering, the little bread and wine that we can spare.

Eleven years of absolute silence before the shadow of Phrixos fell on Haliartos.

Aegidios saw it first, but he did not wake me. He pointed it out to me when I woke. The shadow, deep and dark even in the dark of the outer Aether, troubled me. We searched for a cause of this shadow, peering through the far-eyes. Perhaps some island had drifted between Haliartos and the sun? No, the dim light of the sun still shone on us, and we cast no shadow on the much larger Haliartos.

Perplexed, I checked the tally of days. It was still seventy days before the priests would return. I wondered if this should be reported sooner. I wondered if it was dangerous, if Haliartos was in danger.

We had only one line to Earth. It could be used only for emergencies, and using it would leave us without any ties at all. The priests would be angry if we alarmed them for no reason.

We sent the automaton-ship home.

And we waited as the shadow seemed to move closer to Haliartos. Suffocating it. More fires burned in the darkness, but they were pale and weak.

We realized our error within days. The priests would arrive only a few weeks before they would have, otherwise. The shadow lived and moved faster than that.

Phrixos seemed bent on devouring Haliartos, and we had no way to stop him.

Neither of us willingly slept anymore. We sat in front of the far-eyes and watched the fires of Haliartos die. One by one, as though a giant finger touched each of them and snuffed it out.

We watched as the massive island, cloaked now in shadow that ignored all else to cling to the island, was pulled apart.

Silence. Absolute, total silence. Piece by piece, Haliartos crumbled. A child could not more thoroughly have torn the colony apart. Entire houses were separated from their moorings and set gently adrift in space. A barracks floated past, once, so close that we could see through the windows. The miners were still sound asleep, except for one unlucky soul who hung from a foundation, screaming. His screams were silent. No one heard him.

Stones drifted through the glimmer of the Aether. Bodies. Buildings. Tools. The debris and detritus of humans arrogant enough to believe that they could settle in the lap of the gods.

Aegidios and I sat and watched in utter silence. I have fought in Africa, against the fierce tribesmen. I have seen men gutted and trampled by war-elephants. The chaos and horror of war pales next to this silent, ruthless extermination. The second barracks drifts by. These men are awake; one runs from the door. He does not catch himself in time and drifts away from the barracks, screaming. His hands stretched out to us, but what could we do? There is no help for these men. The priests will not come in time. Haliartos is destroyed.

"This is the gown that *he* would give our Lady," whispered Aegidios, and I was forced to agree. "He will cloak her in the black cloak, and we will all die."

It seemed that the destruction took months. Nothing was left where the island had been, except for a darkness deeper than we had ever seen, a darkness that seemed to have ripped a hole in the Aether itself.

After our shock had subsided into a numb horror, we checked the hourglass. Five hours a turn, turned just before the first stone drifted away. Sand still lingered in the upper portion. Less than five hours to destroy a large, heavily-armed community.

Aegidios fell to his knees and wept. Whether in sorrow or fear, who can say? The harsh sounds of his sobs broke the deep silence. Shocked me. I can claim only that, when one is so accustomed to the depths of silence, madness is the only result.

And so, as he knelt, weeping, my hand closed on the knife that we use to mark the hours. Again, time slowed. Each detail became crystal-sharp. The bust of Chronos carved into the haft. The etchings on the wall, the hours, the days, the months, the years. We have been here for so long. This is our freedom, our prison. We have failed our duties; there is no reason left for us to live. The priests will not let us leave this place.

It was madness that put the knife in my hand and lifted it to the shadows. It was mercy that drove the knife downwards, into Aegidios' back. It was fear that pulled his head against my loins to stifle the sound of his screams. It was love that kept me from howling my own noise, from rending the Lady's tattered cloak further. It was all these things, madness, mercy, fear and love, that brought about Aegidios' death.

He thrashed against me for so long, so long that tears wet my own face. He had become a younger brother to me. My only friend, my companion against this silent madness. He had not deserved such a cruel life, though his death was on his own hands.

I crumpled to my knees next to his body. Shattered life lingered in his eyes, broken hope and terrified love, the knife was too short to penetrate a vital organ. Slowly, he was bleeding to death. Slowly, his light faded.

"Please," he whispered, a merest breath from withered throat. "Please!"

I kissed his forehead and cut his throat, and the blood bathed us both in offering to the Lady.

I carried him to a bed, and brought my food and water near me, and cradled his corpse until the priests found us. The water was gone, by then, the food, rotten as his corpse. I must have reeked of death.

I could only stare as they questioned me, holding scented handkerchiefs in front of their noses.

"Another one," they said, and disgust shone in them, in the light that bathed their perfume-stinking bodies. "Another colony gone, and the watchers too mad to tell us."

"Phrixos," I whispered. "Phrixos has turned his eyes on us."

"See?" said the priest. "They babble about the spirit of fear and some goddess of silence that they have created. Mad, all of them."

He turned to leave, pausing at the door.

74

"Burn it to the ground. Do not leave a splinter standing. When it is done, brush it from the rock and we shall curse it. No one must know that the darkness is spreading."

The acolytes lit a fire in my hearth. They doused our house with oil, and our bodies with it as well. They trod well around me though, to do so. Phrixos's shadow hovered on their shoulders, that delicious fear that he feeds on must have been thrilling down their backs.

They doused us and then laid a trail from the fire. They ran for it, the cowards. We are alone, as we have always been.

Let us be a sweet savor in your nostrils, Lady. Let us be an offering to you, repair your cloak with our ashes and deny that dread Lord your loins for one more day.

Only you know that he has set his servants on us and only you know that he will devour all. He is coming, and he will not be denied.

Blessed be, Lady of Silence. Blessed be, Lord of Fear.

Stone and Starlight

SO IT IS THAT they have come to this new world, this new fortress. Walls of stone and starlight rise around them, binding them to land and sea even as they change it to their needs, and wolves prowl at the heels of a lost king, and the new age mewls its first pained breaths.

We were beyond hope, when the call came. Our seneschals and quartermasters warned of diminishing air and dwindling water. Those of us who could drop our physical forms, did, submitting to being bottled and stored on shelves. Our great powers, useless without the raw material to give them form. Our wealth, useless and inedible in the empty depths of space. Our incredible city-ships, shedding their skins into the endless nights.

We were lost, without hope for safe harbor. Despairing, unsure why we held out hope. Forgotten, cast loose from the wondrous things we created.

And then the beacon, invisible and silent but undeniable. Calling us, dragging our eyes back across the years to the lands we had left. We could not resist.

Over the millennia, you have heard tales of those who left, of those who returned. You will think you heard of us, perhaps, call us gods and myths, but we precede the gods. We *created* the gods. Do you understand now why it was so galling, so *insulting* to be summoned home like errant chickens?

Do you understand why it wounded us to obey? In our youth, we shaped universes and hewed the foundations of the world that you now know. We wanted to resist. More than you can ever imagine, we wanted to turn our backs to this miserable call and take our noble, free deaths on our own terms.

And yet.

Perhaps it was the years untold that broke our spine, or the uncertainty. Whatever it was, this last insult took the breath from us. Where once we would have broken the sky open to herald our return, now we skulked back, slipping to the planet's surface in shame and fear.

The first taste of that air, of that soil, of the sea-spray and dust storms, rain from the mountains. *Fire.* Everything that gave our power shape and life flooded our senses. It burned like fire, our atrophied veins stuffed to bursting.

Our cities opened like flowers under rain, their stale air rushing out of our halls to be replaced by the scent of grass and rain. Our hearts bloomed in power and joy.

We set our anchors deep, ruining cities and breaking lands. This world was ours, once, what do we care if the usurpers have claimed what is not theirs? We are gods. We paid no heed to what lay below.

Long have we rued that arrogance, for when our borders were besieged and our heroes falling like chaff beneath an ill wind, those who might have been allies turned their faces from us and gave us no support.

But we were home, and the walls of our cities shuddered as they settled to earth so that the rebuilding might begin.

Oh, they were sad echoes of what they had once been. Where once proud warriors guarded their proud gates, now debris blew sadly in the winds of our homeworld, the guards moldering in bottles in the Halls of Waiting. We had lacked the resources to sustain so many bodies, or to give new ones, and our birthing chambers were immediately given every possible resource to bring them back to full speed.

Those of us alive so badly needed our kin to share in the glory.

But there was one we did not wish to share this new world with.

When first the great wars exploded across our reality, sparked by bitter gods beyond even our understanding, we built weapons to protect ourselves. Beautiful weapons, built of flesh and soul, imbued with our power and fear. At first they turned the tides in our favor, built causeways from the bones of nightmares cast from the broken gods' bones.

But they were not strong enough in the end, and we were cast loose from our home, the surviving weapons broken and grieving, strangers in our midst.

We did not cease. What limited resources we had were poured into new weapons. Fear drove us. Fear and hate and grief, all these we poured into the bones of new weapons. We gave them the form of children and grew them with dark magic and the despairing memories of an entire broken race.

Only one survived, a thing we later regretted.

We took what we had learned and built a new weapon. A girl in heart, a weapon in intent, a monster in necessity.

We did not entirely expect her to survive.

She did.

We bound her in the dark, wrapping her in dreams and removing her power from her, for we could not kill her, not with what little strength we had left.

We do not wish to share this new world with the deadly child of our despair, but she is waking, and with her wakes the end of our power.

I Am Made of Every Color

SECRET

He found the first one on the floor at the grocery store and asked the clerk about it. "Oh, that's Anna," the clerk said. "She's something. I think God took all the colors he had left and painted her out of them."

Jason laughed at the obvious hyperbole and went on his way. He forgot about it within minutes. Three weeks later, he ran into a woman as he was going into the post office.

The collision knocked the letters from his grasp and a shred of shining skin off of her hand. It rustled onto the street, catching the light. He stared at it stupidly, and then at her face. She was indeed made of every color. Impossible shades of translucent green and peach and pink and gold shone from her white skin. Skin made of the same nacre he'd picked up in the store. She was beautiful. Magical. If the clerk hadn't said something, he'd never have noticed. If the letters hadn't scattered like feathers over the pavement, he'd never have seen.

"D-doesn't that hurt or something?" He was terribly awkward. It was like every time he tried to talk to the co-worker with the lazy eye, or to his nephew, who had Down's. So hard not to stare. He wanted to touch her, see if her skin felt as odd as it looked.

She waved it away. "It was just a tiny memory, I think."

"I worry about all sizes of memories," he said, and invited her to dinner. He had no idea what he was doing, or saying, and didn't realize what he'd done until she was gone, and he had a dozen envelopes and a cheap ad flyer with her number scribbled on it.

He realized later that she must have been terribly lonely, to accept an invitation from an awkward stranger.

MEMORY

At first, it had been in her chest. A tiny lump that formed when she was just about two years old. Her mama had smacked her on the bottom for talking back. The next day, the tiniest of bumps on her chest. Her parents, not inclined to notice little things, paid no attention. But it grew, now and then, when

79

something bothered her. When a playmate called her mean names, when her cat got hit by a car, it grew a little bigger.

She'd turned eight before her mother, giving her a bath one evening, finally noticed.

They took her to the first doctor, who assured them it wasn't cancer. He agreed that it shouldn't be there, but it showed up as normal flesh to all their tests, and what could he do?

"Wait and see," he said.

By the time her first boyfriend broke up with her, it was about the size of a golf-ball, and the doctors were firmly convinced that she was either a mutant, an alien, or a top-secret government project released into the wild.

"It's like pearl," one of them said, "but we can't figure out where it is coming from, and it's nothing—biologically or chemically—like we've ever seen. Her ribcage has actually grown around it." He wanted to do surgery, but she cried, and he reluctantly gave in.

"It isn't going to hurt her, as far as I can tell," he admitted. "It's just a lump, but it's attached to her heart and spinal cord, and surgery would be very dangerous. Let me know if it gets painful, or inflamed, or she has strange symptoms."

"She has a pearl-that-isn't-a-pearl, growing in her chest," said her mother.

"Well, normal strange symptoms," said the doctor.

The girl smiled and stroked the thin skin over the lump.

SECRET

"What's your favorite color?" Jason asked, worrying a piece of her pearl-skin off of her arm.

"Black and white," she said. The skin slipped off, another tiny secret. It would join the others he kept in a box in his office. Hidden from her.

"That's not a color."

"Nope. It's a no-color and an every-color. It's me."

"Your favorite color is you?" he asked, laughing.

"Yep."

"Ok. But why? Why do you turn everything into something else? My secrets are just words in my head."

She shrugged, gracefully.

He kissed her wrist, savoring the feel of nacre that was still hardening. Her outer skin was old and brittle: little secrets, old secrets, other people's secrets. That skin came off easily. He was addicted to it. Putting it under his tongue allowed him to taste things she hid.

"I know why you like white. You *are* every color. But why black?"

She grew very still in his hands.

"Because all of my colors are on the outside," she said.

MEMORY

On her sixteenth birthday, the skin broke. She was alone in her bathroom when this happened. It hurt a little, but the skin was mostly dead, anyways. The rich gleam of a pearl shone through, golden-white struck with green and blue, yellow and silver.

She never let anyone see her chest after that. The boys assumed it was a weird fetish, but they didn't care much. If they touched it and asked about the weird lump under her shirt, she told them it was a benign cyst. Most of them quickly stopped touching it.

Ed was different. He felt the lump, and he wouldn't take that for an answer.

When she bent over one day, he saw the tell-tale gleam from inside her shirt and wouldn't be dissuaded. Since he was her steady boyfriend, and she was a little drunk, she let him take her shirt off.

"Oh, wow," was all he said, before he started kissing it.

They were married four months later, because anyone who loved that most secret thing must love her, too.

SECRET

"Move in with me," Jason said, as they lay in bed together. He'd found a loose piece of shell on her lower back, right above her tailbone. He didn't want her to tell him what this secret was. It would be more fun to see for himself.

"Ok," she said, and pulled his hand around between her legs. "But I shed."

He laughed into her shoulder, playing with her labia. "I noticed."

He sucked on the shell, under his tongue.

MEMORY

Edward loved the pearl more than he loved her. When they fucked, he never kissed her on the mouth unless she asked him to. He kissed and fondled the pearl. When she covered it up around the house, he got angry. If she wore anything in public that would show even the littlest glimpse of it, he got even angrier. He called her "Treasure" and "Jewel" and "Precious," but he almost never used her name.

She got pregnant, and they were happier for a while. Ed forgot his obsession with the pearl...a little.

She miscarried at six months.

There wasn't much blood, but the pearl grew so large that it squeezed against her ribs.

"It needs to come out, soon," said the doctors.

Ed did all of her talking now. Her throat was squeezed shut with grief, and her lungs couldn't seem to quite fill. "How will you do that?"

"I'm afraid we'll have to drill it out," said the doctor. "It's too large now to remove without tearing her apart, otherwise."

"Destroy the pearl?"

The doctor gave him a strange look. "Sir, it is destroying your wife."

"She isn't ready for surgery yet. Let her get over losing the baby."

Ed took her home.

SECRET

She moved in with Jason, with her cats and too many books and not very many pictures. She didn't try to make over the apartment. He was a little surprised. "You live here—don't you want to decorate?"

"I don't know how."

"You haven't ever decorated a place before?"

She hung her head, couldn't meet his eyes. He could have sworn that her glow faded.

"I did, once. It got messed up."

Skin fractures deeply across her chest, and he knows he's found one of her big secrets, one of the secrets around her heart.

He takes her into his arms, but she is stiff and silent. This is a secret that isn't ready to fall off.

MEMORY

She got held up by two small-time crooks, coming home from the grocery store. They spilled the milk and took the ten dollars she had left. It was the last ten dollars they had because she hadn't gone back to work after the baby, and Ed was swinging between jobs, a victim of the economy. He wouldn't get paid for another two weeks.

He hit her, hard, across the cheek, when she got home and sobbed out her story to him. She was already bruised from the robbers, who had groped between her legs and pawed her breasts. She still wore the pad, because it was only a few weeks since the baby, and she was sure that was the only thing that turned them away from raping her.

"They could have found the pearl!" he yelled. "Who would want to fuck you?"

Shocked, scared, tearing apart, she swung back at him, screaming inarticulate, mad-woman griefs. For a moment, he was the focus of all her hatred and hurt. The pearl shrank a little, maybe fueling her anger, and his eyes went cold. He caught her hand and tied it behind her back.

She raised her voice at him one more time, but he taught her a lesson, and the pearl grew again.

SECRET

He became obsessed with finding out her secrets. He teased secret after secret out of her, unwinding her like a mummy. Down and down, although now she cried when she told him her secrets, and cried when her shell sloughed off. Bits of blood flecked her where he sometimes had to pry off the secret. He comforted her, of course, but sometimes he found himself having to bully her a little bit. It was for her own good. Surely the secrets must suffocate her, bind her. If he could pry them all away, she could love him.

"I don't want to tell you. It hurts."

"It's good for you!" he cried, and kissed her on the chest, where the huge, pitted scar twisted her body in a horrifying way, even with its lustrous sheen.

She burst into sobs then, and cowered in his arms, clutching the sheets to her throat. He wondered what secret would be so terrible that even the physical reminder of it was some sort of secret to her.

MEMORY

Ed had found out her biggest secret. Her hurt and anger and fear made the pearl grow. So he hurt her and found a little comfort for himself in hurting her. He knew his life was crashing around him, the cards slowly sliding towards inevitable collapse. He drank, and he gambled, and sometimes the only money was from illegal things, but it was a life.

She huddled on the bed, curled into a fetal position, and stroked her pearl endlessly, until the collapse came.

SECRET

"It's ok!" he said. She had been crying in her sleep for almost an hour, curled into a fetal position. He was scared to touch her. But then, she rocketed up, screaming and flailing at an invisible aggressor, and he caught her in his arms.

"Don't touch me!" she cried, and beat at him. Trying to protect himself, he grasped her arms and shook her gently.

Her moan was like a wounded, tortured animal. She subsided in his arms, limp and unresisting. He felt her skin fracturing beneath his fingers.

MEMORY

Someone started pounding on the front door. She could hear it from her bed, but nothing really mattered. She stank because Ed was afraid soap would damage the pearl and because she didn't care anymore. Ed threw open the bedroom door and grabbed her arm, yanking her off the bed. He hadn't fared much better than she had. Too much alcohol, too many late nights gambling, the inner demons that spoke through his dreams. He had never shared those dreams with her.

"I'm out of here," he said, "and I'm taking you with me."

She started to protest, her voice a weak croak, before she realized. He wasn't talking to her. He was talking to her pearl, the big, luminous thing dominating her chest. It didn't hurt any more, just sat there, one more weight among the many hurts.

He tied her wrists to the bedposts and pulled out his hunting knife.

When she came to, she was in a white room. She was clean. A hospital. Her chest was light, loose, empty.

"Hello, dear, I'm glad you're awake."

It was her mother. She realized she hadn't seen her mother since before the miscarriage. "Mommy..." she said, and tears welled up in her eyes.

Warm arms enfolded her, and her parents held her as she cried.

She didn't need to ask about the pearl. She didn't want to know how she had survived. She would deal with that later.

SECRET

He listened, silent, as she told him her story. This was a secret he was glad he hadn't found, glad he hadn't tasted. The raw hurt in her eyes was enough, the thin, thin skin peeling away as she talked. It would have choked him, torn him open. He held her close, and stroked her shoulders. "How did you live?"

MEMORY

She hadn't wanted to live for so long, but she woke up in that white room, a shadow and a whisper, and found herself clinging to the shreds of her life. The pearl had represented everything strange about her, all of her hurts bound up into a smooth little package. Maybe it was a new lease on life.

The doctors didn't know what to make of it. For her to be alive was a miracle, given the massive trauma to her chest.

Sentenced to six months of bed-rest, she began rebuilding herself, a little piece at a time. She pulled the colors from the world around her and created a protective chrysalis, using her secrets to hold herself together.

SECRET

"That's when I discovered my skin," she said. She was lying in his arms in the dark room. "It started in my chest and filled all of the other cuts and scrapes after that. He had done so much damage that I was nearly in pieces. But I never told anyone how bad it had really been, or who had done it. My parents only saw me after I was cleaned up, and I told them that someone had mugged me, and that Ed was probably dead. When I told them that, the skin started covering my entire body. It was frightening at first, but then...it was right."

MEMORY

With her pearl gone, she found the gaping hollow in her chest gruesome, embarrassing. She wanted to fill it with something as beautiful as the pearl. For a while, she haunted the S&M clubs, dated more abusive men, made friends in the cancer and AIDS wards. But nothing filled her except anger and more hurt. None of it helped heal the gaping wound in her chest.

Then she met Yelena. Yelena was everything Anna wasn't: confident, witty, outgoing, comfortable with herself. Yelena didn't see the holes or the raw flesh; she didn't find anything strange about Anna's skin. They were happy together, Yelena protecting Anna and Anna caring for Yelena.

One night Yelena whispered *I love you* into Anna's ear. The next morning, Anna woke up, her fingers clutched by Yelena's, and felt a little less empty. She crept out of bed and tiptoed to the mirror, lifting her shirt in the dim light filtering through the curtains. The light shone softly red, shimmering through the red gems crusting the hole in her chest.

NO MORE SECRETS, NO MORE MEMORIES

"There's no hole there at all," he said softly, brushing his fingers over the smooth swells of her breasts.

"Every new bit of happiness filled it a bit more," she said, stretching luxuriously. "Yelena and I went our separate ways, eventually. I chased happiness from city to city until I landed here. Over time, it filled out until I looked normal again, as long as I kept the scar covered. Maybe it will start growing like the pearl did. I don't know."

He leaned down, kissed the smooth skin between her breasts. "And here I thought the term was 'heart of gold'."

"Mine's much more valuable," she said, laughing.

He smiled. "Valuable indeed."

Her laughter faded instantly. Reserve shone in her eyes.

He rose up, straddled her waist. Pressed her hands above her head. Fear shone in her eyes as he lowered his head to kiss her. "So valuable, and no one has ever appreciated you."

As she trembled between his knees, he kissed her jaw, her collarbone, her nipple. A loose scale caught his tongue, and he worried it off of her body. A trickle of blood ran down her hip.

"But I do. And I don't want there to be any more secrets between us."

She smiled back at him, her eyes sharp and cold. "As you wish." Bucking, she got her knees into his groin, threw him off of her. He flew backward, stunned, rolled off the bed.

Stunned, he scrabbled at the covers as she rounded the bed, the gun pointed square at his head.

"You should have talked to me, instead of tasting my dirty secrets. You think you're the first person who has done that? Did you ever ask where I worked? Ask to meet my friends? No, you stole from me, over and over again."

"Here's the last secret, sweetheart." She clicked off the safety. "Someone does value me."

Leviathans Whispering of Goddesses

YOU KNEW IT WAS going to be stressful, this family reunion. The cars start pulling into the driveway and you find your shoulders hunched, your head bowed, your focus firmly on the garlic and carrots. You're in the kitchen because cooking and reading and getting out of the house and moving until your legs give out are the only ways you cope. It's the only control you can have in a family of dragons and knights and kings, where men rule and women serve.

It's not long until cooking and reading aren't enough, and the noise and camaraderie of everyone else drives home that you don't belong, that you're the one out of place, marooned all by yourself with twenty years of emptiness on either side. You don't belong here, unwanted stranger, changeling.

More people have arrived, and the pressure is sitting in your throat, driving you out, just out, anywhere out, and every little obstacle builds that pressure until you can't breathe. The beach is right there and you run to it, to the icy waters and wet, clinging sand, to a red sun sinking into the fog, to wire-sharp grass and an endless, calling wind.

And then it's walking, walking without purpose, your anger and self-pity creating a space of surf and seagulls and the dank, bitter waste of alienation from the people who are supposed to be your safe place. The dripping fog and kelp are warmer, safer, than your family, safer than you.

So you walk, letting the things in the dark corners of your soul churn. You walk some more, until the waves feel warm, soaking up to your thighs. Your eyes sting from the salt, the wind, and the anger.

The western sea is where the dead have always been brought, or gone, or said to have gone, tales of gods and demons receiving them, of bright lands and dark hells, just the other side of the horizon. Perhaps it is not only souls that are carried away to the sun, but dead hopes and fears, too, maybe, carried away on that silver path burned the resting sun.

The sea takes all without question, and you wonder if it is enough to cast your fury into the waves, to let it be devoured. You are the child of death. Is there enough death here, enough to lose your anger to the sea, enough to let your soul rest through the long dark night?

Silence has never frightened you. Loneliness is a comfort you do not know how to live without now, and you revel in it, wrapping it around your shoulders like a grey shawl embroidered with shreds of fog and broken shells and the bright flowers clinging to crumbling cliffs.

It is intoxicating, this feeling of being alone as the fog turns rose-gold in the setting sun. The tide rises, and the night chill settles against your lips. Your shoulders ease. A hissing wind seems to fill that hollow in you, lifting your feet above the packed sand. You turn your eyes to the ocean and wonder if you carry enough death, enough grief in your soul, enough emptiness to be a fog-light.

Enough to find that land of heroes and dead gods.

So you go to the silver path. You shed your clothes and your tears and walk into the sea, your feet finding the sun's beckoning finger. You walk beyond the reefs, their sharp edges filling the world with your blood. Darkness swims at the edge of your vision. Leviathans whisper tales of great comets and goddesses tearing the world in two.

You suck in salt, filling your lungs and blood, filling yourself with tears and the trapped souls of kings and slaves and gods. The last drops of the sea dry on your lips and your hair capture the golden light of the sun in a web of copper and pulls it from the sky. The moon is a gleaming opal caught in the hollow of your breasts, and still you walk, following the silver path across the endless night.

Co-Exist

IT WAS THE POLITEST zombie apocalypse anyone could have imagined. Really, we weren't even sure we had zombies, or an apocalypse, but some news guy called it that, and you know how these things take off.

Well, to be honest, we didn't see it at all, at first.

Most of us grew up on comic books, horror movies, and the CDC's zombie-awareness guide. Turns out, the more you see, the more you miss.

Had it been a virus, we would have created a new medicine. Supernatural causes? We have plenty of priests. Maladies of the mind can be fixed, too. We tried every explanation we could think of.

It wasn't...anything.

It had been happening for a while before anyone caught on: people get stuck in ruts, zone out, go missing, have emotional breakdowns, it wasn't anything new. Then a guy got hit by a car, and with a clearly broken neck, tried to keep crossing the road. Bystanders said he'd crossed that road every day of his life, but never...broken.

It took twelve police officers to bring him in, and most of them were wounded.

Once they got him out of sight of the road, he went limp, lost. The emergency doctor examined him and declared him completely brain dead. Judging from the level of neural decay, it had been a while.

They put him in a cell and issued a bullshit report to cover up the incident.

As usual, a few nuts on the internet got hold of it, but they'd been yelling for so long that we ignored them. Then, we started to hear about friend-of-a-friend incidents. The cases were increasing. A dead woman would step out of the body bag, go to the grocery store every day, buy the same items, come home, put them away, feed the dog, and fix dinner. A man went to work every morning, sat at his computer, and came home. Kids went to school. They were all dead, bearing the gruesome marks of their demise. Soon we all knew things had changed, but not how to respond. It wasn't like moaning, flesh-eating corpses were chasing us down the street. They were just...there.

90

It was so bloody *polite.*

They didn't do anything as long as they weren't disturbed. They couldn't be talked to, turned aside, moved in any way from that one compulsion. They walked in front of buses, put out the cat, stood in line in coffee shops—they were just...

There.

Finally, they made the news. The CDC started testing. Now doomsday cults sprang up around the most heavily-concentrated areas. New products hit the market, aimed at the "Unstoppables." Hollywood filmed its first big-budget zombie movie in thirty years. Hysteria, panic, and paranoia set in.

The only ones who didn't lose their heads were the Unstoppables.

Early tests showed some sort of traumatic brain death. No one could definitively say "this is why," but it was—as far as anyone could tell—instantaneous.

Why the routines, the inability to stop? The patterns they followed weren't necessarily the ones they'd died doing, as far as anyone could tell.

And what kept them physically alive? They couldn't speak, write, or engage with the people around them, but they could do complex tasks, if they'd done it often enough.

More tests. More laws and rules and merchandise and TV shows. The neuroscientists found a single, tiny portion of the lizard-brain that seemed to imprint on the moment of death. One memory, whatever had left the deepest groove in their minds.

Well, we knew *what* it was. We just couldn't, for the life of us, figure out *how* or *why* it was. There was no rhyme or reason. No one could predict who would die, making it impossible to study accurately, or to find a cure. All we could do was clean up when we could and study random population samples in hopes of finding something.

Although it proved shockingly resilient, the tiny surviving part of the brain *could* be destroyed (and this is, really, why we called them zombies). But it was hard to make that choice. For many, the idea came too hard to kill your mother, your wife, your child (and the children were the worst, some of them stuck in play or fear or despair) when they weren't trying to kill you. They were too hard to let go of. Some still looked and even acted like someone you loved.

We expected outside forces to do the hardest separations for us.

Humans have always been able to find someone else to do their dirty work. New job markets sprang up. Identifying the Unstoppables, removing them from the premises, providing counseling for the people left behind. Killing or storing the Unstoppables. Churches and faith healers who promised magical results. Memorial-builders.

Undeath became a commodity.

Some of the Unstoppables were caught in nightmares—rape, murder, abuse. Mercy killings were legalized, but only by licensed professionals in conjunction with social workers and psychologists. Others remembered bits of trauma, or their darkest lusts, and preyed on the living. Fortunately, they lacked subtlety and were quickly hunted down. Public service ads targeted on treating our fellow humans with dignity and respect became the new norm.

Afraid of creating monsters, kindness became a law, and a societal virtue, but we were still so helpless.

That was the worst of it. We'd have been okay if they'd been violent, death-dealing, biting, cannibalistic zombies. With the climate changes and sudden plagues and the growing madness of the human race, we were used to planning for catastrophe. We all had supplies, bug-out bags, safe places, emergency plans. We knew how to contain outbreaks and put down riots.

We knew how to fight.

There was no fight. No answers, no reasons. Sometimes we didn't even know if they were a zombie. Panic can only be sustained for so long, and after a few short years of riots and faith-killings and emotional breakdowns, society began to settle back into old routines.

We had to survive, somehow.

So here we are. We've mostly stopped trying to get rid of the Unstoppables. We let them continue, as long as they aren't damaging anyone. We live beside them, shaping our steps and thoughts around their needs. We care for them, wake up next to them, love and fear them. We fear becoming like them. We fear what may come next, wonder what it is like to be one of them.

They consume our thoughts and lives.

They are the fortunate ones because they do not know fear. The worst has already happened to them. Some of us are little better than they, caught in an endless maze of dread and uncertainty. We welcome death, hoping it will be real. Others reacted as humans have always reacted to fear: with color and sound and joyous defiance, or hatred and despair.

We can't fight it.

In the end, all we can do is to go on as we have always gone on. Maybe they will die out. Maybe we will all end up like them with no one to end our scratched-record minds. Maybe a cure will be found, or at least a *cause*.

We can't fight it, but we can coexist.

For now.

Dreams...Now

WE TAKE IT AS a point of pride, my clan, to remember every story that has been told, ever song that has been sun, every name we have heard. Faces and voices are our currency, and we are paid handsomely when we choose to be spies and politicians. We are the lore-keepers, the knowledge-seekers, the story-hunters. We feast on words, and many are the jokes told about the best way to shut us up.

We, of course, know all of those jokes; it is also a point of pride. Words are *good*.

There are many stories from the years of my life. I am the Long Memory, my life preserved beyond even the long centuries of my kind by sorcerous means. I am the bridge between dynasties and generations. Queens and heroes seek me out; scholars travel across the stars to learn at my feet. Before the Light, my name was spoken throughout the universe. The Living Memory of the Dead God, some called me, the Dream-Keeper, the Echo, so many names. All were deserved.

All are now remembered only by me, and by the few students and aides still with me.

So I stroke these pages and whisper the stories to myself as the libraries shudder under the assault of the Light's concussive waves.

94

Exquisite Ghost, It Is Dawn

EXQUISITE GHOST, IT IS NIGHT. *Exquisite ghost, it is night, and I am not alone. Exquisite ghost, it is night, and I am not alone, and yet you are not with me.*

Exquisite ghost, I promised you we would never be separated.

Exquisite ghost, fret not for vengeance, for my heart has broken as surely as my word.

The thoughts flow through me as the cold sand flows through my fingers. The tide approaches swiftly, threatening to cut my alcove off from the rest of the beach. The lovers and families have left, the parking lot is empty of cars, no more dogs chase sticks into the foaming waves. Thick white fog flows slowly from the sea, rolling over green hills and twisted trees.

It is silent, and I am alone. Yet I am not alone, for the memories of a thousand souls linger in my fingertips. Each grain of sand a memory of the stone or shell it came from, a shard of a story. Each handful is a shattered mirror, reflecting time and tale that I cannot begin to guess.

But I am alone in the ways that hurt.

It began when I was young, this loneliness. It was not bitter, then, but blessed relief. The great golden heat of a sun on gleaming hills, the rustle of restless wind in ancient oak, the lonely cry of a red-tailed hawk high above. Heat and wind and stillness, as though every living thing was merely an echo of a distant world. Autumn, with its dry storms and smell of rain on dry dust, petulant breeze riffling a horse's mane. Winter, solemn and grey, cloaked in drenching rain, wind keening at the corners of the house as it fought to come inside.

It was a beautiful silence, a loneliness that settled into my bones and refused to be moved, even when others were present.

I was there, but they were shadows, and now I am the shadow, and they are there. I do not know how that happened, or when, but I am not sorry for it.

A tiny shell catches in my fingers, smaller than the nail on my smallest finger. Bleached white, fragile as a child's heart. It tells me of a tiny conch and a much larger seagull, hermit crabs, and early morning beachcombers. Pitted, its edges notched with sand and stone, it is a sorry thing now.

95

I crush it between my fingers and feel its relief as it crumbles away to become sand.

Everyone needs something to be.

The tide is coming in, and I have combed this alcove free of its stories for now. It is lonely enough that I may take whatever shape I wish to walk the shoreline, but I am caught in memories and two hands are best for sifting stories out of sand.

The wind is the thing I love most about California. I have heard godlings of other places talk about their wind or storm or breeze, but there is nothing like the many winds of California. The wind on the northern coast is heavy with salt, flush with power and curiosity. It will have driven the fog well over the cities by now, the tide of white flowing over Oakland's shipping crates (like great beasts looming over an apocalyptic landscape) and San Francisco's glittering towers, and even Marin's expensive, quiet hills, but it is silent here, for now. I can hear crows chattering quietly in the distance and the low of cattle from the pastures above me. Somewhere, an elk bugles, and I can hear whales singing beyond the cove. The wind will come with the storm, but for now, it is utterly still.

It is most beautiful like this, when the gnarled trees drip fog-sweat onto still paths and even the waves seem muted. Wild iris, purple as king's robes, and yellow lupine dot the hilltops, abstract splatters on the grey-green hills over sheer red cliffs.

It is the sort of day when one might look nervously over their shoulder, wondering if another god will rise from the depths to break the earth and rewrite everything we know, but it is too still for that.

My parents may not have many manners, but they know better than to disrupt this.

This is one of the few places spared the wrath of the Last Night, one of the few places still drenched in too many old stories to crumble to dust under the weight of some hungry monstrosity.

Waves lap on the shores, calling my name. She is down there, in the depths, the Drowning Goddess. She calls me, night and day, and is never so loud as when silence covers my world and everything about me is as echoes in the fog.

The natives of this land used to believe that these shores were sacred, that the path of the sun across the sea at sunset was the path to the afterlife, that Coyote waited to welcome them home.

They did not say what happened when that path was gone, when the sea is flat and grey and sings only of a betrayed goddess.

I killed everyone who knew and drowned their souls with her.

Exquisite ghost, it is not night. Let me go. Let me find my peace. Let me atone for my mistakes and move on.

She is loud tonight, woken no doubt by my memories whispering in her nightmares. I do not try to guess what she might dream there. I dream enough for both of us. I woke for so many nights with the press of the sea on my chest, seaweed clotting in my throat, my body shattered by the endless pounding of the waves.

I did not used to hate the salt water. I stopped sleeping. I can still hear her.

I hold court for myself, sometimes, those days when she has been wailing and I am drenched with guilt and fear. I present my case to flocks of seagulls or curious seals, noisy jurors who no doubt would carry my tale with them wherever they went.

The authorities would, perhaps, wonder over the unmarked corpses littering the beaches in mysterious mass deaths if they were not so busy fighting off things from other realms. I am the least of their monsters to fear. But the seals are beginning to wonder, and the elk, though the sharks have learned to appreciate my guilt. The seagulls would not notice if I sat and killed them one by one, so long as there was food to be had.

I defend my case to juries of seals and seagulls, the crabs and starfish my only audience. I do not know who I think my judge is. Perhaps the sea. Perhaps the wind. One of those will be merciful to me. The other is choked with her tears and cries. I doubt it will judge me gently.

Yet the days when I hold court are few and far between. I did what I had to. She had followed at my father's heels, would have laid waste to everything I hold dear. I could not stop him, but he had bigger things in mind than my coastlines, and when his hunger was sated, he returned to the sea and let his body return to the form it wished. (I am sorry, Montana, for your unexpected salt lake. Be glad he remembers enough to hunger for the things beyond your reckoning, or there would not be enough of you left to resent the lake.)

But her…she was nothing, a minor tributary, an upstart godling who rode my father's crest and thought to use his hunger to find her own legs. She gnawed on my coastline and cut short so many of the stories I had not yet heard, and I caught her by the throat and dragged her beneath the sea, anchoring her with all the weight and hatred of the fallen cliffs and broken stones she left behind.

When I remember the cry of the breaking land, the shattering trees, the drowning people, I can almost forget that I loved her. Almost forget the years she had spent wooing me (I am a very distractible creature, if you haven't noticed yet, and cannot always be bothered to notice love). Almost forget the feel of her waters running through my hills, of the minerals she brought from the mountains and the rich redwood bark. Almost forget her betrayed screams as I buried her beneath the waves and broke her tethers to the land.

In time, she will lose her shape, lose memory of what she is, and gently sink into my father's great mass.

But for now, she screams and pleads, reminding me of the love we shared, of the bright days and quiet nights we shared.

She does not realize that she is not the thing I loved, that her greed and ambition changed her from that merry river I loved into a thing bloated with greed and dead bodies. She claimed what lives she could long before my father rose, and polluted his shoulders with her stench.

She is not the thing I love, but I love her memory.

Perhaps she will be cleansed, deep beneath the waves. I have heard humans talk of the power of salt, of salt water. Tasted their tears, their blood.

Maybe the salt will cleanse her blood, bring back my exquisite ghost.

Maybe the salt will bring back the silence.

Maybe I will sink beneath the waves and break her chains someday.

Maybe I will be able to love the sea again, when it is not bitter with her tears.

Maybe…

Exquisite ghost, it is night. Exquisite ghost, why did you leave me? Exquisite ghost, fret not, for my heart has been broken, but I will heal you.

Exquisite ghost, it is night.

Dreams of Apocalypse

WHEN ANY OF MY clan has taken the Rites of Memory, they are turned loose into the Shattered Realms. They are expected to travel between the broken worlds, finding the stories that survive. A Story Keeper's legacy is memorialized by the number of stories and songs and memories that they rescue.

The daughter of a Lore Writer, the granddaughter of a Grand Storyteller, the great granddaughter of a Story Keeper, the expectations I bore were legendary.

I did not disappoint.

Time moves differently for us. We were born in the concussive blast that birthed the Light. We move between the fragments of its destruction, travel over the soundwaves. Often we reach worlds before the Light and rescue as much as we can from its vicious hunger.

Most of those traveling the realms move outward, looking for worlds where they may make lives, young worlds just birthed. They seek to study myths as they are born, to watch the shape of heresies and faiths unfolding. The new, the strange, the places that will grow and glory in their strength and know the Light only as a soft glow on the horizon for many generations before they begin the inevitable slide into apocalypse.

I turned my face inward. The worlds nearest the source of the Light are wild, burdened with mutant creatures and horrific phantasms. Scoured by storms, by death, by fallen angels, the few survivors cling desperately to tales of a better time.

These are the stories I hunted, and when I returned, I was robed in a gown of tales that rivaled even my grandmother.

I earned my name, but I mourn still for the worlds I walked. If the Light pushes at our walls now, then they are long gone, nothing but a memory in my dying libraries.

The Dream of the Broken God

WE HAVE A HUNDRED names for it. *The Labyrinth. The Corpse. The City. Home. Hell. Heaven. Others in languages your dreams have never heard. That-which-gave-tears. Taste-of-speech. God-corpse. Mother-lost.*

We come from it, wrapped in our own dreams and nightmares, forms as beautiful and monstrous as we can imagine.

You come from it, with your clever hands of clay and your chain-bound hearts. The Elders come from it, shadow and song and the-wind-that-cuts-flesh. The Queens, too, and their children, starlight and stone bathed in blood. Other things, too, each with their own horrors and songs. Gods and Kings made of parasites and scavengers fed on flesh divine beyond reckoning.

You cannot find it if you search for it; it is beyond sight. But if you close your eyes under the full moon and start running, you might find yourself following the opalized veins of its dead heart. Or maybe you'll fall overboard from your fishing boat and discover yourself swimming in its tears (yes, it still weeps, though it is dead). There are many ways to find it, but never when you want it. Only when you need it.

And what you meet there…

We did not all leave. Many of us, those predators who came while the flesh was still warm and the heart still beating, we are different. We cannot bear to leave this thing, though it is little more than bones and a fragile shell now, but we starve in its emptying halls. Endless worlds branch from the dead god's fingertips, or slip slowly between its ribs, and we have tasted them all, but most that taste sweet are too well-guarded. We are not many, those-who-came-first, but we are big, and powerful, and so very hungry. We will not be denied for long.

The Broken God does not like to be found, but we would be happy if you found us. We have riches, beyond your imagining, and secrets. Stories and songs unheard by mortal ear, sorcerous knowledge distilled by the gods of unknowable universes. We even hoard a little of the godflesh still, if you are enough.

Come.

Come to us.

Come through the door.

100

Come to the end of the road.

Oh, how I wish I had never heard that shivering voice. I first heard that whisper as a child, caught in fitful dreams. It lured me to its gate, and even then, I saw it for what it was but gave no sign that I saw its trickery. I was not the only one it had lured, but I was the only one who saw. I became separated from them, the grey powder filling my lungs until I woke, choking.

I did not go through the door that day, but it had smelled my soul. For years, I struggled with the nightmares, my childhood tormented by monsters and ghosts who wished me harm. Whatever foul thing rules this place, it does not like those who see through it, and it tried everything it could.

At first, I suffered, waking each night with the taste of death on my tongue. My childhood disappeared, my exhaustion so thick that I could not tell if I was waking or dreaming until the dreams seemed far more real than the waking world.

Slowly, I grew into my war. I learned to fight, to find the true names of things and spit in the face of nightmares. I grew cold and wily, my spear and neck adorned with the claws and teeth of the things it had sent after me. I had no name, but I was known throughout the Broken God, a nightmare among the nightmares. I had no mercy, no restraint. If it came within reach, it was mine to slay.

For a while, they ceased besieging me, and I found some peace, alone within dust-choked halls, breathing the memories of a hundred lost adventurers. It is no way for a child to grow up, but it is the way to raise a warrior.

Eventually I learned the secret of the Broken God, learned that she was merely the nucleus of reality, the place where all things touched and crossed through each other. I learned to see within her strange bones, to find doors and windows that looked out over worlds beyond my wildest imaginings.

Yet for all that I knew her, I could only look into those other worlds. The doors and windows were barred to my soul. The thing that hunted me had found its weapon: I could not leave the Broken God if I did not have a body to take my soul to the places it thirsted to visit, but my soul could not return to the dreary life it had left behind. It was used to war, to fighting for survival, to seeing enemies in every shadow. The soft things of friendship and physical comfort seemed only to be traps set for a moment's disregard. Slowly, my soul and I grew apart, became separate creatures. I still dreamed of her, but it was no longer my eyes I saw through, but hers.

In the end, perhaps it was inevitable that the thing should get what it wished. Perhaps this *is* why it called me.

Come, then, it whispers, and grey dust huffs from its mouth.

I step within, and my heart trembles, once, as my foot sinks into the sorrow-fine drifts of dust. It brings back terrible memories, rising to coat my mouth and nostrils. Panic overwhelms me, for a moment, as I remember drowning in this. Maybe I did die, so long ago, and my body somehow survived on some cobbled dregs of soul. Perhaps now I am going to meet myself in the afterlife.

Ah well, if I am already dead, what worse can it do to me? Steeling myself with these thoughts, I forge ahead, determined to meet it head on.

My dreams had prepared me for many of the sights I might see—a dragon big as a mountain, overlooking a drowned city, its eyes blinking sleepily as it turns to regard me, caught in a time much slower than mine; a herd of horses under a red moon, their leader white as death, beneath dying cedars clinging to the cliffs of a surging sea; great valleys stalked by venomous spirits of endless winter and valiant witch-queens, were only a few of those strange sights—but it had not prepared me for the stranger things. Waking mind was not meant to see so much of what lies beyond our sight, and my heart quailed against memory of my darker dreams.

For so long, I walked. My legs, used to computer chairs and Starbucks runs, burned and then ached and then went numb. My feet, soft and unused to hard wear, chafed in the dust that found its way into every crease of my skin and toes.

My shoulders harden under the straps of my pack, but I do not grow hungry, and the food I carry rots, uneaten. My eyes…I am glad there are no mirrors, for they redden and weep endlessly, scratched by the cruel dust, and the mud forms a mask on my face, cut to ribbons by my tears.

There are some advantages of being an incorporeal soul.

But there is nothing here that eats bodies. Things brush endlessly against me, but it is not flesh they crave, not my weak, mortal flesh, not when they are glutted on the carrion of a god, and so they do me no real harm.

It is a mixed blessing. I am unharmed, but harmless. My futile swipes at ethereal monsters does nothing. My arm is not practiced for the sword, I know no magic, I possess no great power of courage to burn away my foes.

It is a cruel blow, especially as my heart is still so filled with the knowledge of my soul's conquests. I can taste my power and strength, smell the fear of my enemies as they cower before me, and yet the ones I see with my weeping eyes laugh in my face, inviolate. Overcome with frustration, I wail my fury and beat at them, but they turn to mist and fade away, leaving only the echoes of laughter in my ears.

I am lost, useless, alone, and the foreboding that haunted me, that the Broken God's monster called me here only to mock and destroy me, grows stronger.

For years, it seems, I wander. I discard my pack; my clothing wears to shreds. My shoes fell off long ago. My hair is a matted mess, my face a grey mask ruined with tears. And always, that fell voice in my ears. *Give up. Lie down, find your peace, forget this battle. Let your burdens go; you are useless here. You are holding her back, keeping her from that glorious path she seeks. If you were wise, you would die, if you cared, you would die, if you knew anything, you would die, if you were brave, you would die, if you were if you were if you were die die die die die...*

That, then, is its error. If it had spoken once, left the doubt and exhaustion rot in my mind, tainting everything it touched, I would have succumbed. If it had been quiet, fleeting, taking me off-guard, it would have won. But it was greedy and pushed me too hard, and I have always been one to sink my heels into the earth when pushed.

I do not die. Even cold, alone, hungry, wracked with fever and doubt, I will not give it this victory. But as time passes, I grow less and less sure of my stubbornness, for this Pyric victory gives me less satisfaction with each moment.

Finally, the path peters out into a desert. The cold night sky is empty, the ground a barren wasteland of white sand and tangled black trees with bare branches, as though burned with a great fire. Orange light gleams from unknown sources, as though fire burns in a hidden dimension just out of sight. There is no moon, no life, no sun, no stars.

Yet, for all that this place should terrify me, a deep and alien peace fingers the fringes of my worn mind. It is as though I stand in a graveyard, where there is no more expectation or struggle. I am alone here, there is no one to see or judge me. The air is cold, scented with wet sand and stone, soothing to my parched lungs. Before long, I find the source of the scent—a wide, shallow stream, clear as ice—beneath the trees. Its edges spread across the sand, but its center is dark, unmarred by sand, seemingly without bottom. White stones dot the edges of its bed, partially submerged in the sand. They create tiny ripples, glowing with their own gentle light.

There are no words to describe what passed through me at that moment. I fell to my knees in the wet sand, afraid to sully the purity of the water, desperate to plunge my hands, my face, my very being into it. My first touch is gentle, hesitant, as though this might be a mirage, but it is cold and so very, very wet, so cold it is as though tiny points of fire touch my fingers as I touch them to the sand. Reassured, I can restrain myself no longer and plunge my face into the water, letting it wash away the horrors of my journey.

There has never been a more blessed moment in my life, nothing that could ever compare to the wonder of it. My lips touch one of the strangely glowing stones, and I nearly drown on the scream, for it blisters my skin with its heat on contact. I break off a branch and move the stones away from a patch of stream to protect my feet. I bathe, and the water turns black and muddy with the foul dust, and panic chokes me, for the stream is utterly still, and the water does not clear. Guiltily, I wash the rest of my body and move away from the stain, hoping that I have not angered anything.

In my new resting place, the water is wide and shallow, the trees tangled and thick. A quick search yields a hiding place, a nest to protect me from the unknown things that must surely haunt this. If nothing else, the silence is so full that every whisper of sound I make feels like a violation. I need to be invisible for a while.

My routine becomes simple, comforting. The water nourishes me; I have not needed food since I entered the Broken God. I have managed to gather enough of the small stones to create a heat-source, a blessed luxury, though I was never cold here (but never really warm, either). I scavenge far and wide and finally learn that I can dig through the sand for the rare treasure—a scrap of cloth, a stick, a bead, the flotsam and jetsam, it seems, of a lost world…or more.

Again, time passes silently, in unknown quantities, until a quiet dread begins to grow in the back of my mind. I have seen no other life since I came here, but now it seems as though some great monster steals near. There is no doubt that the source of this dread is hunting me, but I have no name for it, no understanding of what it is or how I might fight it. So I hoard my meagre treasures and build what new life I can in the endless twilight.

It is as it has always been when I finally see the source of my fear—lightless sky, the glimmer of the sand and river-stones, the black trees. A figure strides across the plain, visible somehow between the trees, tall as judgment and lean as winter, cloaked in black shadows and white bone. Creatures follow in her wake, mares red as blood and hounds with glowing eyes, fell birds with wingspans that would have blotted the sun, and flittering things for which I have no name.

But I have a name for her.

It takes her hours to draw near, and I have prepared for her, sitting before a fire that I have kindled from the branches of the trees—they burn hot, but too quickly to use often—cross-legged on the orange cloth-scrap that is my prize possession. My salvaged beads—black and blue, yellow and green, in shapes I cannot imagine or banal as a plastic pony bead—hang around my neck.

She draws near, this terrible, beautiful phantom, and I quail before her, too aware of my stupid, unwelcome self, of the scars I have left on this pristine graveyard, of all my thousand sins.

And yet, I am proud. She draws near, sits by my fires, and the things that follow her fall to boiling flat shadows in the firelight, drawing across the plain behind her. She sits, shadows shedding from her arms, and regards me curiously, hungrily. I meet her eyes, all fear gone, eager for this meeting I have dreamed of for so long.

There is no shock. No connection. No recognition. The thing before me wears my soul, but she is changed beyond recognition. Her face is scarred with the memories of endless battles, her teeth are broken into long, jagged shards, even her hair is weighted with venom-tipped fangs from unknown creatures and jagged pieces of metal that clink when she moves. She is alien to me, and it occurs to me that I should cower in her presence. I am weak, emaciated, aged beyond my lifespan, tired with futility and broken dreams, burned dry by the very water I drink to live, a lost stranger in an alien land, but I have not died, have not given up, and for the moment, that terrible victory is as great as her own.

That knowledge shines in her eyes, envy lighting them for a moment. It is a battle she does not understand, against a foe she cannot slay. Perhaps the only thing she cannot slay, and that burns in her a little.

I have forgotten you, the shadows around her whisper. *I have forgotten our name. I have forgotten what I was.*

I nod, my breath stolen at the sound of her voice. Suddenly, I feel as though I have been breathless since she was stolen from me. Her tone sends reverberations through my heart, waking things I had forgotten could exist, warming my cold blood to new life.

I have not forgotten you, but I have lived a half-life, anticipating this day.

What am I? What are we?

I do not know.

Our voices are effortless, shared thoughts quick as light.

What is my name? It is not our name anymore.

You are not me, anymore, and I am not you, but we are still us.

She nods, thoughtfully, and catches a shadow from her hair, sucking it between her jagged teeth.

My story has been very long, but it is just beginning.

A terrible certainty fills me. I am here to be shed, an old skin to be sloughed off into this graveyard and left to desiccate and become one with the sand around me.

It is time for you to leave me. I am hampering you, holding you back. It is time to shed me and become who you are.

Time to write a new name.

Yes.

She nods thoughtfully, but makes no move. She is in no hurry, she is feared by all, and the nightmares of the Broken God lie quiet under her hand.

You must slay the Broken God's monster for me.

Her look is quizzical, confused.

There is no monster.

It has been calling me. It is what trapped us. I can feel it—

The realization strikes us at the same time, and her face grows sad.

I am the only monster in the Broken God. I am the thing that has haunted you.

I nod, my heart heavy. So many years of torment, of fighting against this creature, only to find it is…nothing.

We share, silently, for hours, for I have experienced her tale, but she knows nothing of mine, until I have nothing left to say, and she has no secrets left to spill.

106

Thank you, she says, finally. *When one holds so many secrets for others, one has no room for their own.*

I will carry them to my death, unspoken, and the graveyard levity brings a quirk to her broken lips.

She stands and puts her hand on my shoulder, turning me to the water. *Look, and I will show you that which I have seen. It is the last secret, the very last secret of all.*

I turn, and as my blood spills into the water, it washes away the sand and drips over a great golden moon before me, and trees as bright as fire over golden grass.

Your blood will open the doors of this labyrinth for the Lost Queens, and we will ride forth and reap the wrongness of all worlds.

Lord of Heaven and Earth

SUPER-HOUSE ENGINES ROARING to life, the Nidhogg shook himself loose from temporary hibernation and stretched his wings. The shockwave flattened the sagebrush and sparse, dry grass. The power stored from a week of hard flight surged through the systems. Lights blinked on, startling red in the colorless sunlight. The non-launch crew grumbled and pulled blankets over their heads.

Outside, the launch crew went through the barely-familiar routine of pre-flight checklists. Well, the practice itself was familiar. It was the Nidhogg who jumbled their routine with all of his new tech and organic modifications.

"We're all clear!" yelled Technomancer Williams. She battened down a final clip and hopped off of the wings. "Wings are cleared for take-off."

She wiped her hands on her breeches and stepped into the cargo bay. "There's some frayed silk on the inner sub-seven. Should last till Atlanta, but we better replace it then."

Captain Scott Janus nodded and drew an orange X on a large diagram taped to the wall. Only one other X, a yellow one on a tail-joint, marred the hand-drawn blueprint of a classic Nidhogg.

"Should get someone to draw a new 'gram," said Williams. "There's so much stuff on him that isn't here, we're going to miss something."

"Got a hand with art?"

"Nope." She shrugged. "Plenty of old techs who do, though."

"You want to let people in on his secrets? 'Sides, it would take months for someone to figure him out even a little. Not even sure who'll be able to do the repairs. We need to get an in-house mechanic."

She shrugged again and took a seat in front of the tech console. "Someone's going to find out, sooner or later."

Janus stepped onto the lowered deck. The early-morning sun blinded him for a moment, until the inner-eye shields slid dark. "Best biosci invention ever," he muttered.

He walked around the Nidhogg. He'd captained Dracul before, the massive half-tech, half-organic warships, but never a Nidhogg. His experience was with the quicksilver Fireflies, the serpent-sleek Sheshas, the half-feral Amalindas.

Never a Nidhogg, especially not one like Prometheus.

Gun-metal scales shone with silky softness, even smudged and scratched from the long, grueling flight. The sinuous neck flung upwards, loosening joints and cogs and bones in a flurry of creaks and clicks.

"Good morning, Captain," said the Nidhogg, lowering his head.

"Good morning, Prometheus." Janus checked Williams' work. He trusted her implicitly. She'd been flying with him since their first classless mongrel-flyer, back during the Rising. She knew the Dracul, inside and out. She would check his work, too.

Never too careful. Not with the Dracul. Not with a prize like Prometheus.

The guns had to be triple-checked. The facial armor had to be applied and strapped down. Lights had to be double-checked, engines and wings checked every time someone turned around. Gears and cogs, intake systems, neural monitors. Claw and landing systems. Thousands of tiny parts, both mechanical and organic.

And the eyes. Eyes, eyes, eyes. The eyes couldn't be checked often enough. Dust or grit sliding beneath the ten-layer silk and crystal shields could blind the Dracul. A blinded Dracul would crash within minutes. That was their one failing. Though their sensors and radars were more advanced than any warship on earth, sea, or sky, the Dracul were still too organic, too easily panicked by blindness.

Janus had been in one of those panicked behemoths. Aeternitas, the Grandship, the Flying Fortress, King of the Skies, the Second. Janus had watched Aeternitas, blinded by acid, claw his eyes out.

Remembered wheeling, falling, wailing.

He and the remaining crew had parachuted to safety and watched as their beautiful, mighty Dracul fell helplessly to shatter on the shores of the Salt Lake. They had laid there and watched Vritra, the rogue organic Dracul, melt the metal exoskeleton around Aeternitas's organic core. They'd watched, helpless, as Vritra encased Aeternitas in a useless shell of warped gears and singed silk.

They'd trekked to Salt Lake City, on foot, in the summertime heat, to look for a mage. All of the mages were in Denver, protecting the walls from the Texans. The crew had stolen a mongrel flyer and flown to Carson City. The mage could only kill Aeternitas. There was no saving him.

Janus remembered that death, more clearly than any other moment of his life. The days, the nights. Quivering, grinding creaks of ruined metal. Flaring arcs of wild energy as Aeternitas' power railed uselessly against Vritra's subtle rape. Aeternitas wailed and wept, voice human and something far older, far more heart-wrenching.

By the end, in the silence left by that last, agonized wail, even the mage had wept. The captain, clinging to the wreckage of the Dracul's head, shot herself before the echo of the scream had faded.

Janus wiped the outer eye-shield with an oiled rag, lost in his memories. He missed Aeternitas. The ancient Dracul, battle-scarred and mighty, had carried them through the Rising. He had turned the course of the battle and saved the West Coast from Imperial Rule.

Even Prometheus did not have the weight of presence, the power of the old serpent.

Janus flicked a grit of sand out of the corner of the eye. It swiveled, focused on him. Janus smiled, weakly.

"Everything feel good?" he asked the Nidhogg.

The great eye blinked, once. The signal for yes. Though Dracul emotion could not be read through their eyes, they projected well. Tentative concern prodded him. Prometheus could not speak while Janus was clinging to his face. Too easy for the human to fall to the ground.

"I'm okay," Janus replied. "I'm okay."

Janus climbed down and Prometheus shook his head carefully, testing the tightness of the straps.

"Tighter on the nose-line," the navigator said over the PA. "It's chafing at one of the visual sensors."

Janus climbed back up the rigging and tightened a strap of leather wider than his thigh.

"He says we're good!"

Prometheus lowered his head to the ground, allowing Janus to clamber down. He patted the Nidhogg on the cheek and jogged back to the hold.

"Batten down the hatches," he said. "Let's get to a real way-station tonight."

The wastelands of New Mexico stretched away to the mountains, painted black and white by the young sun above them. Prometheus paused for a moment in the harsh white sun, his organic tongue flickering, taking in the subtle, myriad scents of his world.

"Preparing for launch sir," the navigator reported, and Janus strapped himself in as the thrusters under the engines began to roar.

"You've got that shit-eating grin again, sir," the technician said.

"Always gonna," he said, and flipped a switch to seal the cabin doors. "No way this can get old."

Intercontinental flights had been obsolete by the time Janus was born. Their national unity becoming a distant wish, and the threat of failing fuel resources, life in America had shifted back to a more local pattern. Gradually, the coasts established their own empires, and the rest were left to fend for themselves.

Besides that, new and frightening things haunted the earth, and there were times when technology went abruptly haywire without warning or recourse. Staying close to home became more attractive every day.

The images of those old jets had appealed to Janus as a young boy. His grandfather had flown some of the last fighters, before fuel became more precious than blood. Janus grew up with stories of the thrill, the danger. It was in his blood, and captaining a Dracul was more than he had ever imagined it to be.

The new era had brought challenges that threatened to shut technology down forever, reducing the majority of the world to third-world status. But pockets of resources remained, and these became the locus for war after war. Instead of trying to find a way to expand those resources, to better life, humanity did what it had always done: it expended the last bit of known resources to create bigger, better war-machines.

Prometheus and his fellow Dracul were the pinnacle of those war-machines. Genetic engineering had failed. Brutal, uncontrollable monsters were the eventual result of any tinkering. But the Apocalypse—as everyone referred to it now—had brought them one thing: myth. The myths were too powerful to subdue, too unique to clone, too intricate to tinker with. But many of them were caught in decaying, starving bodies that were too big to be supported by an ecosystem that was struggling to survive.

The dragons taught the humans how to exploit them. It was their only chance to survive. Humanity gained terrifying new weapons, and the dragons lived.

The Dracul had been born from necessity of man and beast. Flying war-machines, blended from the finest meld of beast and machine. Metal beasts equipped with intelligence, with cunning and emotion and loyalty.

Taking off in Prometheus must be like the pre-Apocalypse jets had been, or so Janus imagined. The chassis shook from the power flooding through it; the control panel twinkled and glittered as he and Prometheus ran through diagnostics and system checks.

But Janus didn't think the old jets opened their mouths to roar happily as they took off. He didn't think the old jets would zig-zag through the air like a puppy chasing a ball, just because they could.

Prometheus finished playing and set his course for Bloomington, New Texas Republic, and Janus realized that he was laughing.

In a perverse way, he was glad for the Apocalypse. It had opened his skies.

The lights of Bloomington flickered uncertainly on the horizon, shrouded by the fog rising off the bay. The continental upheaval that had broken America in half had spared the little town and brought more oil to the surface. The New Texas Bay provided port for ships laden with supplies that could be trucked overland to Santa Fe or Denver, the only thing that kept those cities in contact with the outside world.

"We've been given permission to land, sir," Morgan reported, punching a button on the console. The navigator, recently transferred from a decommissioned Amalinda, still had the tremor of uncertainty in her voice.

Janus nodded. "Prometheus, set a landing pattern for East Field according to coordinates."

An agreeable hiss of static answered him and the wings shifted. The Super-House engines slowed, and the Nidhogg lowered, sweeping along the runway. Wind-generators spun backwards to create drag, and steam-thrusters slowed his headlong rush. With a jolt, his feet connected to the ground. His wings tilted. Broad-side to the wind, the huge sheets of metal and engineered steel-silk braked him as he galloped down the runway.

A final shift, the wings folded and tucked gently to the side, and the Nidhogg stood calmly, steaming from the exhaust ports as his engines powered down.

"Well done crew, well done Prometheus," Janus said, and unfastened his seatbelts.

Technicians and orderlies came running with their scanning gear. Landing at any officially-recognized way-station required a full set of diagnostics and scans, and Prometheus submitted to them with bored gentility.

"Super-House class Nidhogg Prometheus III certified clean, ma'am," a technician reported to his supervisor.

The woman nodded and raised her radio. "Hangar C, prepare to house Super-House Nidhogg Prometheus III," she ordered.

"There anyone else here tonight?" Janus asked the woman, climbing down the ladder. Williams would take Prometheus into the hangar to be unharnessed and tended. Janus had paperwork to fill out. He felt so very fortunate, in a certain irked sort of way. At least there were still way-stations that could require paperwork. Most of them, like the one that they had planned to stay at the night before, had been burned out by Apophis and Vritra.

"We've got twenty Fireflies on permanent station," the administrator replied, "and Veles landed two days ago. He'll stay until the damage to his wings is repaired."

"Rogues?"

"Yeah, some new nuisance out of the mountains. Pirates captured an Amalinda breeder a few years ago, seem to be breeding some weird variant, probably with Apophis. Now they want a Nidhogg, I guess. All the cities have pulled theirs back, doubled their escorts."

Janus sighed. There were simply too few of the larger classes of dragon still in the control of the city-states. There were plenty of Fireflies and Amalindas, smaller and weaker creatures that had bred indiscriminately in the hidden places for decades.

But the Dracul—the Nidhoggs, the Tanises, the Sheshas—these were rare, beyond priceless. As new territorial lines were drawn in America, the Dracul were becoming even more desirable.

The highest, most delicate inter-state government contracts weren't made in money or goods, but in the hours of service one government's Dracul could provide to the other. Since the creatures were alive and sentient, yet another level of complexity layered into the equation. Entire branches of government had sprung up around the politics and rights of the Dracul.

And here he was, the captain of a Nidhogg with no alliance or allegiance.

"Your life is about to get a whole lot more dangerous, Captain," the supervisor said. "Belynda was struck down a few months ago during an attack on Atlanta, and repairs are rumored to be impossible. Have to create a new frame for her. You are the only free agent on the east coast, and nobody knows where you are, so word will spread like wildfire, especially in that behemoth."

Janus groaned, following her into the office. "Do me a favor, don't report me until you absolutely have to. I'm already worried about making it back there in one piece."

"Got it. I'll lose the paperwork for a few weeks. Firefly kits steal enough of it on their own."

Janus grinned, but paperwork was suddenly the least of his worries. Like a pretty girl at a dance, everyone would be trying to seduce them to their side now...or kill them.

Veles, a smaller variant of the Nidhogg class, snored. Captain Allie Iglesias sat on the beast's metal nose, her bare feet swinging gaily between his nostrils. Janus met the captain's eyes, and they erupted in a fit of laughter.

"Haven't been able to convince him to leave it off," the captain admitted ruefully. A petite woman in her late forties, Allie was a top pilot and an activist for Dracul rights and privileges. "Drives me bloody fucking nuts, so he'll keep it up."

Laughter sparkled in her brown eyes, a welcome relief from the subdued mood that had followed them east. Allie still wore her pretty floral skirts and white blouses and grease around her nails, looking just like the girl he'd met in the Academy.

Janus laughed, knowing well that Prometheus would do the same if he thought of it. "Still basing in Margate?" he asked, following her to the back of the hangar.

He paused by the burnished copper-tone scales the Nidhogg's head. Veles twitched an eyelid and peered fuzzily at the intruder for a moment before the snoring resumed. The noise shook the entire hangar and vibrated the ground under Janus's feet.

"Nah, got too dangerous there. New boy, name of Kai. Got some big ideals about rivaling Atlanta and Philadelphia, but some weird-ass religious leanings that aren't making him any friends. He's a vicious little prick." Allie was nearly yelling to be heard above the rumble.

"The Kendalls are gone?"

"Jordan's dead, Devin's holed up in a rebel camp with Jordan's daughter and about a hundred refugees. City's primarily underground now, had some really bad disasters."

"Any Dracul in Margate to watch out for?"

Her lips thinned. "Rumor is, Apophis and Vritra stop in there sometimes. But, no room for a Drac in city limits anymore, too dangerous outside."

"I'd been planning to take cargo from Houston to Margate on the way east."

Allie caught his arm with such force that he swung around, staring at her. "What?"

"I need the money if we're going to survive in Atlanta."

"Keep him as far away from Margate as you can, or you're gonna find yourself and your beastie slaves to Kai."

"But there's nothing between Dallas and the East that's safe."

"Anything's safer than Margate right now darlin'," she said, shaking her head. "Apophis and Vritra've got free rein out there now, with Veles and Belynda grounded."

"Texas is going to get cut off if Margate isn't safe for travel."

"Veles and I are going west," she said, "soon as he's mended, to open a way-station between here and Denver. The West's got all Organics and the supplies to keep them in the air. Denver's been isolated from the East for so long that they're sending a squad down to help us hold it open. Wouldn't hurt to switch back to Western support. The East is getting hairy."

They ate dinner together that evening, musing about the Rising and the years since. They had been flying together, he training a young Sheshas, and she providing support and guidance with Veles. They were the ones who had overheard the rumor of a wildly-advanced Nidhogg in Mexican control. A simple campfire tale at a way-station on one of their long flights.

A simple tale that had turned into a three-year mission, the death of a

Sheshas and twenty long-term crewmembers, and the loss of everything that Janus had worked so hard to build.

Janus told Allie as much of their adventure as he could remember, from the first sight of Prometheus to the challenge of fighting the reclusive Southwestern vigilantes.

"We're all that's left," Janus said. "An army went with us to get Prometheus, and they all got killed, except for a few Dracul who are still recovering in the West. But it wasn't even the Mexicans that hurt us. Was the damned Revelators."

"Was it worth it?" asked Allie.

"The Mexicans have the deserts and mountains. I don't even know how long the Organics have been awake, but the Mexicans know how to take care of them, how to grow them. Prometheus...I don't know where they got him. But they treated him well."

"Why'd he come with you? More money in Mexico," Allie asked. "They treated him good." She poured them a little more whiskey.

"He said he was bored, wanted to go home. He wanted to fight, but they were keeping him grounded until they were done shaping him."

As the evening progressed, the topics grew darker, slipped back to the days of the Red Sun—a time now only myth to most of them—and the changing of the world since then.

Cheered by the rare opportunity to talk to a fellow captain, especially one of the few who had run Draculs as long as he had, it was almost dawn before Janus said goodbye.

Allie caught his arm again as he prepared to leave. "Two of the Kendalls are still alive, Janus. Bad blood between us now, so they won't have Veles, but they need a Dracul bad."

"Thought Margate wasn't safe?"

"Isn't. Stay *out!* But Jordan left a daughter before he died, a hell of a little war-witch if I'm not mistaken. Devin's not worth a shit, he's broken and done. If Margate's going to be retaken, got to be her. Prometheus is..." She hesitated, turned away. "No, forget it."

He caught her arm. "Forget what? What have you found out about him?"

"Just take him to Angel's Crest. Keep him away from Margate, from the big cities. He's a pawn to them. He'd be a god to the refugees."

"You told me to keep Prometheus out of trouble."

"I told you not to be stupid. You've been gone for a long time, Janus. America's still tearin' apart at the seams. These ain't the times to stay out of trouble. You've got the best thing there is in the skies, use that power, 'cause the gods aren't gonna save our asses."

"But a girl? How old is she?"

"Twelve, and an older soul I've never met. Try her, Janus. See if they've got the heart left. They need help."

Janus laughed until his stomach hurt. "Allie, are we talking about the same clan? The Kendalls. Black Jack and Ax, the worst gangsters and madmen of our generation? Vicious to the bone, all of 'em, the daughter can't be any better. Why do you want them taking the city again?"

"Because they may be criminals and hell-sons, but they know the place. They're magicians. We need Margate open, Janus. We need the Kendalls there. It's cursed ground, and they know better than anyone how to keep it alive. If Kai's got it, Hydra's got it, and that means that Apophis and Vritra will be able to take over the continent, given enough time."

Janus studied her for a long few minutes. "I trust you, Allie. I owe you. We'll go into the Wilds, get around Margate if we can. Where are we aiming?"

"A place called Hungry Valley. Valley's all weird, but there's landing space on some of the ridges. The Kendalls are on Angel's Crest, above the valley." She rummaged through her gear, pulling out a notebook and jotting down numbers and directions. "Here's your path. Stay out of the cities, fly high, watch out for Organics."

He put the paper in his pocket and kissed her cheek. "Safe flights for you and Snore."

Allie laughed. "You too," she said, and watched as he returned to his Nidhogg.

"And may the gods protect you from him," she whispered.

Prometheus was alone when Janus came back.

"Change of plans," said Janus, waving the paper.

The Nidhogg lowered his massive head, settling it near his captain with a metallic clatter. "We will not be flying to the east?" he asked, the auditory translator echoing a touch in the warehouse.

Janus shook his head. "Allie said there's something up north. Wants us to go offer help."

"You trust her?"

"Always have. Margate's been taken by some cult, Kendalls are gone. Since that's somewhat important to the trade in the area..."

Prometheus blinked, acknowledging. "We must take back the city."

"You don't mind then? There's danger. Too many Organics out there to be sure we'll make it. And pirates. Vritra."

An alien ripple passed across the metallic face, through the robotic eyes. "And storms, accidents, frightened people, politics, other Dracul, assassins, coups and skies only know what else," teased Prometheus. "It's all rather thrilling, really."

After twenty-plus years of working with the Dracul, Janus had thought himself immune to their surprises, yet Prometheus continually surprised him. On impulse, he pressed his hand to the scaled nose and grinned.

"You're just an old Victorian adventurer in a dragon's body, aren't you? Alright brother, we'll see this one out together."

"Will the rest of the crew come?"

Shrugging, Janus opened the access door and stuck his head inside, looking for his gear-bag. "They will if they want a job."

Prometheus's laugh startled Janus into cracking his head on the doorway. Rubbing his head, Janus backed out and glared at Prometheus. "What?"

"Adventure! Fear, fire, foes! We might even miss tea!" said Prometheus. He laughed again, a deep rumble of shifting metal.

Janus shook his head. "And here I thought that they'd neglected your education."

Together, they laughed, and the walls vibrated.

"What's so funny?" Williams asked, coming into the hangar with the navigator and two other crew-members.

"Have a seat, and our brave captain will tell you everything," Prometheus announced in stentorian tones. He rolled his head, slinking it close to Morgan. "But beware, for this is not a tale for the weak of heart."

Morgan and Williams blinked and looked from Prometheus to Janus, who was choking on his laughter.

Janus shrugged. "Don't ask me, he started it."

Prometheus swung his head to Janus. "There Captain, they are ready for you to talk."

"I'll bet they are," he muttered.

Looking vastly pleased with himself, Prometheus settled into a resting position, his nose propped on the floor.

And when the rest of the crew arrived, Janus did talk.

Bloomington faded in the distance as Prometheus set a course according to the coordinates Allie had given them. Settling into a flight-path high in the heavy clouds, Prometheus dampened every heat signature possible and drifted silently through the sky, riding the air currents.

The only chance they had was to disappear off the map. So Bloomington Air worked with them as if they were flying to Dallas, and then slipped them all the help she could on the side. They had registered a false flight-path at Bloomington and hugged it until they were out of radar reach.

A sweeping turn, a thrust of power sent a shock-wave through the air, and Prometheus was off to the north.

Janus unstrapped from his seat and went into the weapons-bay. Allie and the Administrator had sold or given him every weapon they could scrounge, leaving themselves with just enough to ward off an attack.

Everything from buckshot for Prometheus to heavy artillery for the rebels was stashed here, giving them another reason to avoid detection. An unregistered Dracul with this much weaponry would be summarily disabled and both Dracul and captain court-marshaled. The patrols did still run the routes, quick fleets of Fireflies slipping from rock to hill, under the eaves of forests and wrapped in clouds.

Janus checked weapons bindings, nodded at the gunners, and went to the bunks. Williams had found an old war-witch, Michelle Henderson, at the base, and hired her for the journey. Janus sought her out now to ask about the danger of the Organics.

"She's sleeping sir," Morgan said, drawing him aside. "She's been through some rough things getting here."

Janus raised his eyebrows and led the way to the common room.

"She was Belynda's war-witch for a few years, came to a disagreement with the captain and left. I'd say she feels responsible for Belynda's failure."

"She tell you this?"

Morgan shook her head. "The Administrator did. Michelle was on her way back from a stint in Denver studying the Organics when she heard about Belynda. Apparently she was sick for weeks."

"As long as she can fight now."

Morgan grinned. "That, and better. She's one of the foremost human experts on the Organics."

"We'll need that," said Janus.

"Looks to be about ten of them, hatchlings probably, sir," Williams reported. The unmanned drone—barely larger than a crow—buzzed through the rocky outcroppings below and gave the crew a visual of the pride of young Organics basking in the white sun.

"Prometheus, can you see this?"

An agreeable static hiss.

"Any ideas?"

A less-agreeable static hiss, and Prometheus's voice came over the line. "The dominant males in the area are mostly sons of Apophis, the females are ferals, equivalent to the Chumana. These won't be able to fly probably, although they run fast."

"Then we're in Organic territory for sure."

"We've been in Organic territory since we set wing out of Bloomington," Prometheus snapped. "The Dracul do not claim territory, but the Organics snap up every bit they can."

The edge in Prometheus's voice sent a chill through Janus. "Will you be able to tell if there's a dangerous Organic within range? Before it hits us I mean?"

The static hiss again, equivalent of a shrug. "Depends on the Organic. Apophis and Vritra can be in the middle of a city, and you'll only know it if they get careless."

Janus looked at the screen again as panic filled him for a brief moment. What had possessed him to come out here? There wasn't any back-up, no one to receive a distress signal. The Organics loved collecting Dracul parts in their hoards, and humans were delicacies.

"Get hold of yourself, Captain," warned Prometheus. "If there's a chance of making it past Margate, I'm it."

Damn the creature for reading him so well, thought Janus, but he nodded. "Of course. Keep high, power down everything that you can to avoid detection. Silent sonar on."

Gears and engines whined around him, screens shutting off. The drone remained on-screen, an eerie white glow cast around the cabin. As they left the immature Organics behind, Janus saw one young male, larger than the others, raise his head to peer at the sky, his blue throat startling even in the washed-out light of the sun. Vritra's child. His throat burned at the thought of that treacherous, beautiful serpent.

"Stay high Prometheus, and watch out for storms. Vritra has been around."

Another static hiss, and the Super-House swung upwards.

The weather worsened throughout the day. Lightning flickered against Prometheus's sides, the feeds showing blue light webbing his metal skin. Heavy winds on the plains finally forced the navigator to recall the drone, leaving them ground-blind, although the rain had reduced visibility to a few feet, even for the drone.

The gunners readied the weapons, afraid to load them prematurely in the wild weather, and everyone sat tensely on the edge of their seats. Only Prometheus seemed undisturbed. His engines never caught, no static filled the lines.

Hours later, Janus sent the drone back below into the lightening rain. The winds had subsided and lightning no longer touched down. A visual of the area showed them flying to the east of the burned-out husk of Oklahoma City, tornadoes riffling through the wreckage like abandoned puppies. The city had been one of Vritra's first conquests, his nest for years before he became a prime target of every city-state and alliance on the east coast. Now the shell of the city was a hellish wasteland, haunted with thousands of ghosts and throttled by the captive storms Vritra always wrapped around his territory.

Prometheus veered a little farther east to avoid the city. Nestlings still squatted there, squabbling over territory in a strange, endless turf-war.

"Captain, we've got a sighting!" Morgan called a few hours later, punching buttons on the console. The drone-feed magnified and Janus leaned over. A red blip in the corner indicated that Prometheus was paying attention too.

Long and serpentine, a white and blue Organic slithered through the air. No wings sprouted from her back—and the delicacy of her horns clearly indicated a female—yet she rode the air and storm with an ease that even Prometheus must have envied.

"A Sheshas broodmare, sir," Michelle said, startling Janus. He cleared room for her at the console. "The red along her back, a sign that she has young and is not available to the males."

"Is she dangerous?" asked Janus as the sleek Organic coiled up on herself and surveyed the plains.

Michelle nodded. "She can be. The males have huge territories and will defend those, but a broodmare settles on her territory as soon as she can defend it, and never leaves."

The Organic looked skyward and the drone slipped close enough that a blue tongue could be seen flickering as she tasted the air.

"Vritra is rare for his kind, sir," the witch said. "Most of them will defend territory, but not attack like he does. Unless she feels we pose a threat…"

"Load weapons!" Janus roared into the intercom. "We've got an Organic coming at us, broodmare class Sheshas!"

"Sir, wait!" the witch cried, catching his arm. "Don't fire yet, she may simply be curious. Organics seldom care if another passes through their territory."

"She could inform Vritra."

Michelle shook her head. "Not likely, sir, the breeders have little to do with the warriors and barely speak to the Kings. This one is young. No more than a concubine to a warrior at best. Vritra's Queens are the only ones you would have to worry about. But if you killed her, it would be known by every Organic in the nation."

"Hold fire till order," Janus said, reluctant, and focused on the screen again. He marveled as the female slipped through the air, climbing without visible aid. She really was a thing of exquisite beauty—all of the Sheshas were—and deceptively delicate.

She broke through the clouds a few hundred feet west of Prometheus and he slowed a bit. His head dipped, a submissive pose. She ruffed a little, a thin white membrane half standing around her head, warning him off, but offered no further challenge. In fact, as they moved through her territory, she began playing with the huge Nidhogg, looping her long body around him and nipping at his metal sides.

Steadfastly ignoring her invitation to play, Prometheus kept steady, and she soon grew bored, leaving them alone in the sky again as she plummeted towards the ground in a free-fall, pulling up scant feet from the earth and whipping off in another direction.

Mesmerized by her acrobatics, the crew lost a little of their fear. "She's stunning!" Morgan cried as the female skimmed along the river, raising plumes of water.

"And those love-nips she gave your beast would have crushed a man into pulp," Michelle reminded them. "She probably doesn't know about the Dracul, and be grateful for that."

The flight-path required nearly a day's flight to detour a safe distance around Margate. Without way-stations or friendly outposts—Apophis *had* succeeded in razing this part of the country—Prometheus conserved every bit of fuel he could. Lights were kept low; crew-members layered on whatever clothing they had as the temperatures dropped. The wind-collectors hissed and hummed, feeding raw energy into the converters. Prometheus set his wings and glided through day and night, keeping his pace slow enough to detect any threats.

The hours stretched endlessly, the crew clustered around the instrument panels, the guns, the heat-vents.

"The land is angry," Michelle whispered suddenly, sometime in the night. "Its rulers have been cast out, its soul is corrupted, ravening dragons rule it. It bears man no sweet will."

Williams shivered, her eyes glued to the screens showing the ground. "What could the land do?" she asked. "It's just…land."

Michelle laughed and laughed, and finally patted Williams' hand disdainfully. "Oh child, the land is the true Queen here. She always has been. That's why America died. That's why the world died. She got tired of us."

Janus shook his head. "We're not touching down here anyways. Nothing friendly in this quarter on land or air."

And as the white sun rose stripping away the soft illusions and rest of night, the skies did indeed become unfriendly.

"Sir, there's something big over to the east. Organic I think."

Prometheus hissed assent, altering his course to the west.

"Ready weapons," said Janus, and turned to Michelle. "Well?"

Her eyes were already closed, her right hand slightly raised. As he watched, her lips parted, her tongue flickering at the air. He shivered, seeing the resemblance to the Organics she had studied for so long.

"The wind moves with him; his scent is strong on it. The Lord of the Skies is coming."

Vritra. Only he, of all American dragons, could claim that title. Sure, Aeternitas had tried, and the half-decayed skeleton in the Great Salt Lake bore testimony to how well that had worked. Anzu had almost succeeded, but in the end, he was driven back to the Old World, dripping black blood into the sea.

Apophis, black-hearted, ancient, wise, and cunning, had tried to wrestle that title from Vritra in a duel of words, song, and claw. Apophis was Vritra's first lieutenant now, cringing whenever his master came near.

Janus remembered hearing the tale of Vritra's second-known kill in America. A young female Dracul, one of the first hybrids. Vritra had seduced, tortured, raped, and dismembered her while the crew watched helplessly from within her. Vritra had left a few humans alive. The others, he had devoured with relish.

Vritra. Lord of the Skies. King of America. Father of Serpents.

The cries of the fallen Aeternitas thundered in his ears again. Janus's throat dried and he tasted vomit. Prometheus was the greatest of the Dracul, the son of the Fire-Bringer—the first dragon to wake in America—a new breed in his own right, and...a shadow of Vritra's power. Hybrid against Organic.

"Sir?" Morgan asked, her clenched hands as white as her face. "What do we do? Can we avoid him?"

"No," Prometheus's voice came over the speakers. "We cannot avoid him. He has scented us, and he will overtake me within moments."

"Don't fight him!" Janus cried, punching buttons. Override, redirect, deploy cargo, deploy lures, distract distract distract!

Prometheus laughed wildly, shutting down the systems that allowed his humans to control his movements. Metal purred against metal as his huge wings unlocked from their glide. They had to grab hold of handrails to keep on their feet as Prometheus changed course.

Janus swore. Dracul were not able to override their protocols! They couldn't be hacked, and they couldn't take control away from the captains! That was the safety net, the ritual, everything that kept the relationship between the Dracul and the captains possible.

But Prometheus was flying to meet Vritra head-on, and Dracul and warwitch were laughing madly together.

Janus grabbed Michelle by the shoulders and shook her. "Stop him, you idiot, he's going to kill himself!"

The laughter was gone, a cold glee in her eyes. "Vritra's found you, he ain't stopping. Least one of you has balls. Let him go."

Janus shoved her away and yelled into the intercom. "Stop, damn you! You can't win! I'll lose you and watch you die like Aeternitas died!"

Prometheus's snarl was low and primal. "He is a blood enemy. I am the King of the Dracul, and he is their blood enemy as well. It is my duty to kill him."

"You aren't strong enough!"

The world dropped away around Janus. He was in darkness. Without footing. Without ceiling or wall. Empty. Bitter cold chewed into his bones; wind cut gashes in his cheeks. And something massive and primeval surrounded him, coiled around his mind and body. The power shifted, and a golden-red eye opened, and Janus stared into the eyes not of a Dracul, but of a King-Dragon.

"In the world of serpents, the rattlesnake is most feared in the West. Yet the King Snake hunts and eats them." The massive eye blinked once, slowly. "Vritra is my prey today. You will have your revenge, but do not stand in my way."

Janus cowered from the knowing in those massive eyes. None of the Dracul were supposed to have true power, to be able to meet the Organics in a show of every sort of strength a dragon possessed. The blood and bones of the Organics were their magic, something never replicated in the Dracul. The Organics had souls; the Dracul did not!

But this, this was power! This was a dragon! It should not have been possible! He would have sensed it, something would have been said.

"They did not put me into a body," said Prometheus, "they put the body into me, shaped and changed me to be the pinnacle of all things."

The coils eased around him a bit, and Prometheus raised his head, towering above Janus. "Tell your crew to ready the weapons. Whether Vritra falls or not, he will never forget this day."

Janus was back on the bridge. His teeth chattered helplessly and he fell to his knees now, retching. He was dimly aware of a soft cloth wiping his mouth, of being helped to a chair.

Prometheus wasn't Dracul. He was King. He was going to punish Vritra.

"Ready the weapons!" he cried, jumping to his feet. "Vritra's going to remember today!"

And I hope we live to remember it, too, he thought, and took a seat at the console.

Prometheus flew slowly, powering up the piezoelectric Super-House engines to full absorption and switching on the wind-generated turbines.

Only the shock-waves of his wings could be heard in the hold, thumping against his sides.

Flicking on the video screens, Janus connected to the armory. "Listen to Prometheus—deploy the moment he commands it."

"Yes, sir!" the gunners replied, throwing grinning salutes. Ralph, the shorter of the pair, bounced to his bank of Copperhead G30s and checked them for readiness. Close-range armor-piercing rockets, the Copperheads could unearth a bunker or dent a Dracul. Knife-nosed, they would cut through the hide of even the Organics to explode deep inside, and their remote-controlled functions meant they could be recalled if they missed.

Ralph tossed a thumbs-up over his shoulder and Mike shook his head. "Lemme throw Ralph at the son of a bitch, sir. He'll do more damage."

Janus laughed, glad for the banter.

"Hold on," Prometheus warned. A little red light blinked on the console: Claws deployed. Five-foot long claws of tungsten steel scythed through the air on dragon-bone legs, weapons twice the size of Vritra's.

Janus switched on the drone feed and brought it in close to record the battle. If they didn't make it, the drone would go to Angel's Crest and replay the scene, give the rebels some idea of Vritra's weaknesses.

Vritra filled the viewscreen, long and white and furious. He coiled in the air and his mouth gaped. Shock-waves buffeted against Prometheus, knocking the drone wildly off course, the war-cry of a jealous King. Magic—magic that no Dracul was ever able to call—rose in shimmering streams from the patches of blue at throat, horns, chest, belly, and genitals to surround him in a crackling blue shield. Janus knew with sinking certainty that the Copperheads would malfunction before they ever hit flesh.

And then Prometheus screamed and swerved, and there was no more time to think or know. Only time to hang on and pray that Prometheus had not misplaced his pride.

Slashing at Vritra with his heavy tail, his talons raking through the white dragon's magic and gathering it up in handfuls, Prometheus dropped on Vritra. Vritra shrieked too, in pain and rage, as his shields were ripped, and he struck, snakelike, coming away with a mouthful of alloy scales.

Twice Prometheus battered against Vritra, using his weight to his advantage to keep the white dragon off balance. His claws scored the Organic over and over again, Vritra's ineffective legs scrabbling for purchase against Prometheus's slick scales. Battered and harried, Vritra threw his magic at them, buffeting winds, lightning and storm against Prometheus's sides. Greedy teeth of unnatural blue lightning dug at Prometheus, opening gouges along his neck and haunches.

Now Vritra was on Prometheus's flanks. Prometheus screamed as Vritra flung himself in great coils around Prometheus's body and struck like a snake.

Prometheus screamed, furious and hurting as Vritra choked on another mouthful of metal...and blood. Magic seeped into the air around Prometheus, black and venomous. Another terrible scream, and Prometheus set his wings sideways against the wind, turning all thrusters to reverse. Rising for another strike, Vritra slid forward and was flung off. He rolled through the sky in long coils, flailing.

Then Prometheus swept away, his engines and wings straining as he fled Vritra, and the white screamed in victory and chased after.

"What's he doing?" Janus yelled.

Michelle raised her hand, hushing him as her eyes closed. The cabin grew bone-chillingly cold again; the blue mist filtered through the walls to collect in the war-witch's hands.

Prometheus keened, a long, wailing note, and the crew covered their ears as Michelle joined in. Eerie, grating as nails on chalkboard, they wailed together.

The black mist filtered through the walls. It mixed with the blue, swallowed it, and changed it until a net formed of black-hearted blue strands.

Michelle opened her eyes and smiled as Prometheus plunged around a hill, Vritra on his tail. The Dracul's secondary engines boomed to life, braking him. Vritra dropped underneath, twisting to rake at Prometheus's belly with his lightning.

Michelle flicked her fingers. The net dropped through the floor.

Vritra screamed and twisted, clawing at the filaments twining around his body. More black mist fell from Prometheus's claws, and he spat a mouthful of it at Vritra. Blue and black warred over the white dragon's hide, the black opening rents in the blue. Blood, deep blue and thick, welled from long tears in Vritra's hide. The Sheshas screamed, and his cries echoed through the hull with all the power and fury of an ancient, dying god.

Janus watched, his mouth dry. "Can you kill him now?"

"No," Prometheus said. "He will not die without battle that would kill you, too. But I can do other things."

The world blurred as Prometheus dove at Vritra. Claws glittering in the white sun, Prometheus spread his talons and drove them deep into Vritra's body, a roar of pain shaking the Dracul as the magic penetrated into his own body. Prometheus ripped free, taking chunks of meat with him, dripping blood and power as he soared upwards to fall on his enemy again.

With a cold heart, Janus listened to Michelle and Prometheus singing together. He understood Allie's fear. He understood his mistake. He could betray the great dragon, reject his power, or he could accept what Prometheus was: a predatory god, flush with youth and power and fury.

They were trapped, watching helplessly as the King-Dragon mauled and harried Vritra. Streaming blood and blue mist, Vritra gave up his fight for supremacy and locked with Prometheus, fighting for survival.

Disengaging to pounce again, Prometheus shook Vritra loose and spiraled upwards. The white dragon plummeted towards the ground, caught himself, and coiled, hissing at the stooping Prometheus.

Vritra was gone. Leaping out of his coil with a speed only a Sheshas could conjure, he fled towards the river.

"Choose, Captain," said Michelle. "Choose if you will be the first council to the first Drac King."

Her eyes were not unsympathetic. "Choose. Call him from the fight. He will listen. He loves and trusts you."

Janus's finger hovered over the com button.

"Choose."

His finger mashed on the button with desperate decision. His voice was dry. Something squeezed his chest and throat shut.

"You can't keep up with him," Janus managed to say, "and we're running low on energy. Turn. Let's go to Margate."

The King raised his head and screamed a war-cry, the sound shimmering in visible waves. Dirt exploded from the ground. Clouds changed shape from the force of his cry. Prometheus hovered, daring any to challenge him.

Vritra was gone.

Faced with a King-Dragon who wanted to stay and claim territory, Janus reached into his old bag of tricks. "Prometheus, Margate is still their nest. You need to go to Angel's Crest, help the rebels destroy Hydra, remember? *Vritra is Hydra.* There's nothing you could do that would hurt him more."

He watched the drone-screen breathlessly, waiting for the hulking Nidhogg to listen to him. He breathed a sigh of relief when the arched neck softened, when Prometheus lowered his head to lick a dripping wound on his chest.

"We go to Angel's Crest," the dragon agreed. "And when we are done there, Vritra is my prey."

A breath rushed out of Janus's lungs, an exhalation that loosed fear and grief and hope all together. They were going to war. Together.

Massive, curving wings lifted Prometheus toward Angel's Crest, blood streaming behind him. As Janus watched, that blood slowly dripped to the earth. The land would know Prometheus now. It remained to be seen if it would answer his call.

"The land is changing," Michelle said softly. "He has Territory now, marked in the blood of the defeated and the victorious Kings."

"What have we unleashed?" Morgan asked, her face bloodless.

"Change," said Michelle.

The Greatest Hunger

DERECHO BACKS INTO HER corner and huffs, watching her opponent. I can feel her assessing its weaknesses, the deep gashes on its pale, dripping belly, the broken antler. Its other antler is still proud and streaked with Derecho's red blood, but its intestines must be barely held in. A little green blood trickles down a tusk, into her mouth, and her deep-set eyes gleam ruby under the bright lights, vivid against her black hide.

I set my jaw against a rash move—Derecho is too expensive to risk in a kamikaze, blood and glory run—and gather her focus. Time to kill.

I still remember the night this mess started. Las Vegas. New Year's Eve. 1946. The night was desert-cold, a thin dusting of snow on the ground. The city was on watch, waiting to see if the monster that had wrecked Reno was on its way north. I was huddled in a doorway in a bad section of town, trying to keep warm and out of sight.

It was a strange new world we entered, when the war finally ended.

Hiroshima and Nagasaki had been the first salvos, a few months before, the beginning of the end. For a while, everyone thought it was over. But that was just the beginning. Project Manhattan had been compromised so quietly that no one even knew it...until London, Washington D.C., Berlin, and Rome exploded in great gouts of cancerous fire.

We never figured out who was behind it, but it put an end to the aggression. Stunned, horrified, desperate, we turned our eyes inward to repair our ruined world. We found a fragile peace, dependent on depleted resources as much as brotherly love. We were still living under the terror of nuclear fall-out, waiting for winds to shift or another mysterious strike. An air of hysterical hedonism clung to everyone, from New York to Tokyo to Johannesburg, according to the news. The Roaring Twenties looked like a pale omen of the Raging Fifties, silky and gilded compared to the macabre glory of now.

And then, in a final, crushing twist of fate, the monsters came. Drawn by the blood and death and war, birthed by unholy science, they fell from the skies and rose from the seas, unearthed themselves from ancient caverns and crept out of dark forests. We lost almost as many souls to them as to the war, and we quickly learned the fear and respect our ancestors accorded the unknown.

The first ones were small and cancerous, more a danger to individuals than cities. These, we could blame on the bombs. But they got bigger, and science was suddenly at a loss. We knew we had a problem when something huge and tentacled rose from the sea and stormed through Boston. (Maybe Lovecraft was prophetic, if a little geographically-challenged.)

Our communications were rebuilding slowly, so it took us a little while to find out we weren't the only ones. A monstrous reptile had rampaged through Tokyo. A hundred-foot anaconda was killed in Rio. A six-legged water buffalo...thing... was being butchered for its meat after taking out nearly half of Johannesburg's business district. Japan called them *kaiju*. We called them monsters.

Being American, we also called them profit. Even nuclear winter couldn't take that away from us. The war-lords, coal-kings, industrial princes, and oil barons had more money than they could burn. They paid big-game hunters to lead expeditions to bag the biggest trophies in the world, but a house could only hold so many of those.

John Goodnight, heir to a vast silver fortune, financed the first Blood Pits. Four millionaires paid hunters to live-capture the biggest *kaiju* they could get their hands on and pitted the four against each other. The event raised millions of dollars, and Goodnight more than recovered his investment. The next year, Japan had its own Kaiju Wars, supposedly also financed by Goodnight, who had bought heavily into the decimated nation.

That night in Las Vegas, I proved that some of us had been ruptured in ways you couldn't see.

A horn wailed from the police department. It used to be there to warn us about incoming bombers—not that any ever came near Vegas, but you couldn't be careful enough. This time, it was warning of a bigger threat. Take cover. Bombs don't hunt. Bombers screamed overhead, the regional guard heading to intercept the beast.

When the dying Hellcat clawed her way into Las Vegas, her body riddled with bullets and missiles, I didn't have anywhere, or any will, to run. Her yellow eyes, mad with pain and fury, glared down at me, ready to inflict some of her suffering on the creatures who had caused it. I thought she was the most beautiful creature I'd ever seen, and I cried for her pain.

I don't know how, but I talked to her, and she understood. Laid down right beside me, her dying breaths blowing my dirty hair away from my face, and passed away next to me. They found me with my face buried in her blood-matted fur, sobbing.

The hospital patched me up, but within twenty-four hours, I was back on the street, hiding from the newfound celebrity. The bounty hunters found me less than a week later, and only chance threw me into gentler arms, saved me from government interest. Nikolai Kuznetsov paid over two hundred thousand dollars for me, and put me in the arena with his beast, the Drakon, and won the Blood Pits. Charles Goodnight's agent, Mason Kincaid, bought me for two million two years ago, to handle Derecho. We're undefeated.

The Blue Hurricane was the first celebrity *kaiju*. Derecho, eight Blood Pits removed from her predecessor, is the latest.

Derecho's hooves shred the hard-packed earth as she charges her victim. The crowd is deathly silent as the slime-thing spits poisonous goo, but it doesn't slow Derecho a bit, and her gleaming tusks bite deep into the thing's belly, ripping it open. Steaming green guts gush to the arena floor, and Derecho roars her victory.

Back in the catacombs—the Goodnight Arena's monster-holding area—Derecho slumps to the straw with a weary sigh. Whatever her opponent spat was caustic, and she has burns all over her back and haunches. I can feel her pain like a vague burning at the back of my mind, and it annoys me. The monsters are dangerous, but there is no need to make them suffer for our enjoyment.

I have two boys helping me, scarred young street rats who will risk their lives for a warm meal and a roof over their heads. They already have the tub of ointment waiting, painter's poles for the hard-to-reach areas, and softer brushes to clean the wounds. I put my hand on Derecho's snout and lull her into complacence while the boys start cleaning and mending.

I am exhausted when I leave her, wracked with pain and the ashy collapse of adrenaline. I don't know how many more of these fights I have in me. She may be a beast, slow and dull, clouded with the fumes of rage, but how much of that is her captivity, her fear? And, too, there is the darker bitterness against those who sit in their boxes and feed on the misery below, the slow wearing of their bloodthirsty glee.

I am not so far removed from the creatures I shepherd. I didn't come from wealth, didn't learn fine manners. I taught myself to read, to write. I have no grace, no charm, no beauty worth a man's money. No gifts to buy myself out of their pits. Would they glory in my pain, too, if my mutations were visible? Treat me like the gladiators of Rome, goading me with cattle prods and whips, feeding me the barely-dead meat of my horrible cousins?

Why do I ask myself these questions? I am certainly too tired.

"What do monsters fear?" my captor asked me, the night before he sold me to Kuznetsov. We were sitting in a seedy motel room, eating cheap take-out food and lukewarm beer. He had been one of Hellcat's hunters, the first to see me, and he'd saved me from the bounty hunters. My gifts didn't work on him, and I was tired of running. It was a relief to be sitting there, eating my first real meal since the hospital. "How do you make them obey you?"

I didn't know. I still don't, but maybe I am starting to understand.

The door to my hotel room is locked, but I can smell him, waiting. A monster waits for me, a monster I have called, wished for, lusted after, invited through my door. He knows what I am and does not fear me. There is comfort in that.

I am still locking the door behind me when his breath touches my neck.

The next day, her burns freshly crusted with scabs and healing skin, Derecho paces restlessly in her huge pen. She stops, occasionally, to root through the dirt with her tusks, some dim, racial memory maybe of when her kind ate roots and leaves. Dust clings to the drying blood along her mouth. I hope they did not feed her yesterday's kill. It was poisoned beyond use, but they do not always have sense. If she falls ill, I will flay their minds myself. Derecho has become precious to me.

I let myself into her cage, and she comes to me, snuffling concern. The top of my head comes barely to her knee, yet she comes to me and lowers her giant's head to look me in the eye. I hope no one is watching; it should not be known that the animals love, not fear, me.

She thinks she is protecting me, a mother sow defending her child.

A few minutes to calm her, then it is time to gild myself in my garish costume—the purple and gold of Goodnight Industrial, low-cut and tasteless— to take my place beside the other Shepherd. I don't even know who we're fighting. I had more important things to think about last night.

133

My assistant kneels in front of me to begin buttoning my dress, and, for a moment, I am overcome with a memory of the night before. The bruises on my neck ache, although they don't show, and my back aches with the weight of the monster I called.

He is like me, invisible in his mutations. If the people around us knew, would they pick up torches and pitchforks?

I was the first of many, but we are sheep in wolves' clothing, as unlike the others as they are unlike the Silent. (We call them that because they have no voice except the crude one in their throats, ungainly and unlovely, unlike the smooth-flowing stream of our own communication.)

The assistant finishes the last button and crisply adjusts the gold lace over my breasts, lays the heavy gold-and-amethyst Chain of Bond around my neck. It is a circus, and I am the invisible ringmaster, dressed the part of the clown.

The contempt in the girl's eyes is palpable, and I nearly reach into her to squeeze that smug superiority out of her, but the crowd roars, and I can feel Derecho's fear seeping into me.

Of course they would pick up pitchforks and torches if they knew about me. After all, they burned my kind in the Middle Ages, didn't they?

And those unfortunates couldn't do half of what I can barely refrain from doing with every breath.

Another battle, nearly over.

This Shepherd was too weak to repel me, and as Derecho savaged the hurtful thing, I toyed with him. He is a Balm, meant to keep his charge passive. He doesn't understand the sharp, bitter joy of killing, but he watched his beast's desperate battle with a half-smile, enjoying the pain it suffered, and so I took his limp little mind in hand and chained him to his beast while Derecho broke its legs, bringing it to the ground.

His scream should not have pleased me so much. I was not wounded enough last night, not brought to heel. I hope it is that, rather than my greater fear: that my bloodlust is growing, that I will lose myself in the need for death. There is too much to do still, too many things to protect, too many delicate manipulations necessary.

And Shepherds die all the time. They are weak. The weak do not deserve to live.

Derecho crushes the other beast's chest, and the joy of the Shepherd's death tears through me like an orgasm.

Again, I have barely closed the door before rough hands have locked my wrists in front of me.

"You killed him." His breath is hot and dry. He is not as huge as my young memories painted him, but his compact power easily dwarfs my wiry strength. Struggle is pointless. "You killed the Shepherd for pleasure. You are losing control."

Reflexively, I poke at his mind, try to prod him into the actions I want, but I fail, as always. Somehow, I cannot get into his soul to twist and tear and destroy. I have never met another—man, beast, or monster—capable of withstanding me. He is my refuge, the one who knows what I am, who can stop me if I can't stop myself. He kept me safe from the bounty hunters that night in Vegas, delivered me safe to a place that would protect me for my monetary value, if nothing else, and I still sometimes indulge myself in his protection.

I cannot touch his mind, but he can pull my soul out and sate it with violence and the knife-edged pleasure of being helpless again, of not worrying over the powerless, deadly beasts who speak in my dreams every time I sleep.

It is the semi-finals. My costume is more transparent than before, the thin silks clinging to my legs, heavy with golden beads that provide more concealment than the cloth. I am maskless, a brag by the barons that they have the money to filter the air sufficiently, even with all these people. I loathe these costumes, flimsy and fragile and expensive.

I am a free woman in name, but I would never have achieved that if I hadn't struck a deal with Goodnight Industrial: freedom in name, so long as I signed away my life in service to their sport. They couldn't breed or sell me, but neither could I leave, and I could never work for anyone else, even if the Goodnights retired me.

It isn't much, but it is better than many people have, these days, regardless of skin color or gender.

135

I should have specified the right to choose my own costumes.

Derecho is wearying. She will have a full day between this bout and the next—there is no question that we will win and move on to the finals; Goodnight Industrial doesn't keep me for nothing—but she must have some rest.

Derecho's tusks will be gilded on Saturday, for the finals, but today, they gleam a soft, waxen cream under the harsh lights. We groomed her well and showed her affection, bolstered her flagging spirits. She does not understand, but she will fight.

Her opponent is alien, I'm sure of it. I haven't seen her, but in my head, she's sleek and sharp as a razorblade. Doesn't need a Shepherd, probably can't actually be held by one but restrains herself so she can torment him. Poor kid. He is real proud of himself, how easily he tamed her when she was found. Sociopathic fuck. Just waiting for him to get boring. The doctors probably can't explain what is eating his body and mind, turning him into a puppet. Not all the monsters are worthy of my pity, but I do appreciate the irony. I will not abide competition though, and this one...

...this one's angular white head flies across the arena, torn whole from her neck. Derecho is wounded, badly, raining blood and panting in exhaustion, but I am glad of her victory. The alien beast is not something I want in my head anymore.

I finger the chain around my neck, disguising my disgust as nerves. Two more days. One more fight.

"You should be committed."

My punished body is limp and quieted, but he has not, for some reason, left. We have played this deadly game for four years, since I was old enough to want a man in my bed, and he has always left as soon as possible.

"Whatever are you talking about, Hunter?" I stretch languidly, but he growls and grabs my jaw, dragging me up face him.

"I hate this world as much as you do, but you are mad to think you can change it."

Ahh. That. The playfulness flees, bloodlust nibbling the corners of my mind again.

In the aftermath of the apocalypse, those few fortunates who maintained control of the most necessary resources—oil, steel, guns, copper, food— leveraged their power to turn themselves into fat parasites on the broken backs of humanity. I'd lost count of how many soldiers I saw wandering the streets, those few times I was allowed out, missing arms, legs, souls. How many broken hovels housed how many families, how many slaves powered the dawning age.

"It is a madness worth indulging, if it changes."

"You would alert them that our kind exists."

"Maybe that's the plan. We've hidden behind our cousins long enough, made them suffer while we stayed safe. We're not much better than the barons."

His powerful hand tightens even more. He is making speech difficult. "It wouldn't end for them just because you put us in harm's way. You think you'd be a free woman if they knew? Think you'd have those beautiful gowns and the luxury of choosing your bedmate?"

I envy my bestial cousins. Some of them can spit fire, and I would dearly love to melt him right now. "Maybe they won't be around to threaten us."

I beat my fist into the bed and sit up, heat burning in my eyes. "I *hate* this life, hate making the beasts kill and die for someone's momentary pleasure."

He holds me for a minute longer, before pulling me into his lap and kissing me deeply. "What can I do?"

My gown today is cloth-of-gold in an outlandish style, the sheer bodice beaded with purple and pearl, my hair caught in a net of gold wire, a filigree of gold covering my face. The weather reports are good, the wind blowing any contamination away from us. Today only, the roof will be drawn back, the public will be welcomed into the cheap seats, and I will shine in the hot sun like the vengeful goddess I am. My hunter stands in the shadows, protecting me in case I miss a few dangers, ready to bolster me if I encounter unexpected resistance. He is no longer my escape, but my consort and right hand. He fears that I am not prepared for what I will unleash, but he will stand with me.

Derecho senses my turmoil. Her tusks gleam as brightly as my dress, her little eyes squinting, dazzled by the sun she hasn't seen since her capture. Perhaps she knows that she will not be the one on display today.

The band is lively, the crowd eager to see the monster. Charlie Goodnight takes my hand and leads me onto the platform, facing the crowd, and introduces me. His smart cream suit and burgundy ascot do nothing for his doughy face, and I can only imagine how awful our costumes must look next to my fellow Shepherd, who wears the yellow and green of Hercules Oil. I am briefly annoyed, as Melusine, the HO monster, is a beautiful, draconian beast, but devilishly hard to manage, as I recall. I would have preferred Emma Innismoth's privately-owned beast, a tentacled, horrific monstrosity who struck fear into human and monster alike, but was relatively stupid and tractable. Ah, well.

The brass band strikes up; the introductions must be done. I am already deep in the other Shepherd's head, although she doesn't seem to know it yet. I am similarly curled beneath the waking minds of every luminary in the crowd. The commoners may or may not survive, I really don't care. It is the bright and beautiful I will collect today.

"What do monsters fear?" he'd asked me that day, sitting next to me in Nikolai's office. My lip had been split a few days and was oozing again, and he'd wiped it away, gently, and given me water. I realize now that he wasn't much older than I was, making a living, hiding as best he could in plain sight, the hunted masquerading as the Hunter, comforting the monstrous Queen in the garb of the slave. Looking back, I can appreciate what brought us together.

"Monsters fear nothing," I'd said, but now I knew better.

The stage is set. I step away from Charlie, a strange, thrilling certainty stringing through me.

They fear the greater evil, and today, that evil is not tentacled horror from the depths, or blood-stained hell-pig, or beautiful, mythological monster.

In each mind, I stretch. This is the first time I have unfurled my full power. Even I do not know what I am capable of, or what other monsters are hiding in plain sight. I relish the possibilities.

Monsters fear waking to something worse leaning over their beds, reaching from between the stairs to grasp their ankles, pulling that one critical tile from their empire.

They struggle, no more to my power than wiggling worms on a hook. One by one, they rise from their seats. Melusine's handler opens the cage door, as does Derecho's. Melusine will not hold for long; she is slippery and fractious. Derecho is curious, the fog of battle cleared from her mind. This is what I was made for.

Perhaps it is the most fearful who scrabble the most power to themselves, creating shells and buttressed walls of influence and wealth. Perhaps they forget that this armor is a thing outside themselves, but they never forget that empty space just a breath below their feet.

I puppet-march the Kings and Queens of the world to the killing floor, for me kindred to feed on, and in their blood is painted retribution, and revolution.

Monsters fear what we all fear: that someday, they will find that they are not the sharpest teeth, the greatest hunger, the most dreadful nightmare.

By Blood and Fang and Song

MY DREAMS ARE FULL of yellow gas, red mud, green lasers. Blue eyes clouded with death, orange fire swallowing the forests. My days are white, and black, and the washed-out memories of colors, like old, hand-colored photographs. The white sun, born in human war, called the myths from their sleep, and our world was transformed. I do not guess whether it is a better world, or worse, but it is ours, and it is ending as we speak.

The darkness of it is peaceful, the pale wash of white light, soothing. The shadows never leave, rising from the soil in shifting waves. The white sun leeches the color from the day; the red moon casts smears of bloody light at night. It is beautiful, in its way.

The end began on a sunny weekend, when an ancient spirit rose from the depths of the sea and devoured everyone it could reach, including my family. This was only the first terror, the first sacrificial massacre. Governments cried "terrorists!" and "religion!" and went to war over everything and nothing. I was six when it started, ancient when it ended. The monstrous things were hungry then, and angry, waking from their deep sleep and breaking free of their chains. Now they are sated and lazy, searching out only the most tender morsels, and so we keep our cities small and live alone.

The things we somehow called up or released could not be put back to rest when the war was done. We've never figured out how, or why, or what. It just is, and we live with it, and we hope that someday we will wake up to a world that is not wrong, but we do not hope for much else.

I fought in the wars. Twenty-seven years of them. The few of us who survived became deathless, our bodies untouched by years but our minds cowed with age and memory.

Ours is a world that has been jarred from its moorings, unbound from the laws of physics and left at the mercy of imaginations. Gods and demons rise to summons, or their own will, and move across the face of the earth, primeval monoliths, leaving only destruction in their wake.

It is not a gentle world, yet still beautiful, and I had found a place in it, with some sort of peace. It was the eye of the storm, and the peace was not to last.

And so, on a hot, breathless night, I looked north and saw the future.

My parents had died on that beach, in the first attack, and the rest of my family—my uncle and aunt and cousins—had died sometime while I was away, leaving my home empty. When I returned, the horse herds were nearly wild. Some of the old mares remembered and came to me. So I devoted my time to them, raising the foals and selling them to the highest bidder, but sometimes also to people who were as broken as me. Sometimes old soldiers and young children found solace in the herds, and I sent them on their way with a bit of hope. It was all I could do, all I had the will to do. I should have died and had not. It was no longer my fight. We would live, or die, and nothing I did would change that.

I should have known better.

The cedars murmured in the hot wind that night, the herds moving restlessly across the pastures. This heavy feeling was not uncommon before the first storm of the year, but it was too early and too warm. I'd brought my dinner onto the deck, eating ungracefully with my fingers as I watched the horses. It felt like demon weather, though they usually stayed closer to the cities where they could feast more easily. Nonetheless, I loaded the shotgun with blessed shells and spent an hour renewing the protective wards. After settling everything, I took a blanket and my gun out to the smallest pasture, where the high-blood horses milled. I tossed a few piles of hay out for them, and one for me, then curled up in the hay to sleep. The Ghost, my bone-white warhorse and herd stallion, stood watch over me as he had done before so many battles. The dogs, big and black, bedded down in the hay pile out of reach of the stallion's hooves.

Sometime late in the night, I woke, drenched in sweat and shaking in fear from unremembered nightmares. Unfocused and panicked, I thrashed free of the blanket and caught the back of my hand on The Ghost's hock. Expecting him to strike at me, I rolled aside, but his attention never wavered, his long ears pointed away toward the north. His mares and foals clustered off behind him, the mares as still as him. All of the horses, and the dogs, too, were looking north.

The moon, on the opposite horizon, left no explanation for the livid orange glow rising from the direction of the huge lake to the north. The eerie silence struck me then, heavy and oppressive. The shadows seemed deeper.

One of the dogs whined softly, breaking the spell. The Ghost snorted hard, then bugled. The other two herd stallions answered him first, then the five young bachelors. The herds moved, reassuring themselves that their foals were safe. The Ghost, bone-white and alien, seemed to float through the strange light as he checked on his darker mares.

The glow did not abate, ruining my theories of a meteor strike or other natural phenomenon. I should have settled the horses down and gone to bed, but something hot and urgent drew me helplessly forward.

The Ghost came to me as I opened the gate to the pasture. He had carried me home from the wars and was as touched with agelessness as any human warrior. We'd been together for so long, and I had only ridden him for joy since, hoping he would never need to work again. He touched his nose to my cheek and followed me to the barn.

He was easy to saddle and bridle, and stood quietly when I slipped the gun into the saddle holster. I filled one saddlebag with feed for him, then ran to the house and packed a change of clothes and food for a couple of days.

The Ghost waited impatiently, shifting his weight as I secured the saddle bags. Perhaps he had grown as stale and restless as I, and longed for adventure because I was barely in the saddle when he trotted off, aiming for the road.

The roads were ruined by years of neglect, maintained only for horses, and although we passed an ancient Jeep around sunrise, we had the highway almost to ourselves. The Ghost and I were both a little soft, despite our daily rides, and had worked up a solid sweat by the time we reached Hangtown. I had hoped to speak with the sheriff, but she was out answering a burst of violent incidents. Her son didn't know anything about a light up at the lake. I left some money and instructions for the horses' care with him. He'd helped me with the herds during foaling season, and he would watch them until I returned.

For a moment I wondered if I had, perhaps, imagined the incident. Mounting, I gave The Ghost his head, expecting him to choose to return to his mares. Instead, he turned right on Mains and resumed his trek toward the lake.

The oak trees gave way to cedar and pine, and the scent of bear clover filled the air as The Ghost crushed it under his hooves. It was nearly forty miles from town to the lake, on top of the thirty odd miles we'd already traveled.

A brief stop at a rest station mid-afternoon to feed and water him, and then onward. Rested and refreshed, we indulged in a brief gallop along a groomed section of road, racing two kids in a souped-up truck that bounced off of every lump in the road, while The Ghost ran easily beside them with laced ears and a flagged tail. I waved at the kids as they took the exit to Alder Creek. It was dangerous for them to be so far out on their own, without any obvious heavy weaponry or protection. Our region was safer than most, but not enough to forgive such carelessness.

Not for the first time, I wished that the dangers were still human.

It was dark by the time we turned onto the trail to the lake, and I dismounted, leading The Ghost.

The glow was still there. It filtered through the trees as we approached the water, throwing long shadows behind us. The Ghost's ears were back, his pale blue eyes rolling. Something had spooked him badly. I don't use magic often—too many memories of battlefield desperation—but I cast a wide circle around us, protection and shadow-dispelling. The Ghost settled, his nose by my shoulder.

We broke through the tree line into the wide meadows around the shore, and the glow resolved itself into a single, strong shaft of deep-gold light rising straight from the water, a softer radiance diffusing around it.

The Ghost watched nervously as I stripped and bundled my clothes into plastic. I liked to be prepared. Time to find out what had called me here. The water was cold, but not numbingly so.

I swam close, and suddenly the light was too bright, brighter than anything I'd seen since before the war. Blinded, I was sucked down, screaming, expecting to die. Water rushed into my lungs and everything went black.

I woke on a nightmarishly vivid shore. Green grass, yellow flowers, blue sky. The color was garish, frightening. For a moment, the sounds and smells of war roared over me. Then the smell of rich earth enveloped me, calmed me, and I could look upward again.

The sun was huge and yellow, soaking into my skin with a clean warmth I had almost forgotten. The air was clear and crisp, smelling only of good, living things. And it was day. Had I been out that long? It didn't feel like it. I had been out for hours and days before, and I knew that feeling.

I dressed and took the first path I saw through the trees.

There was a town on that path, toward evening. Tall, bright, clean. Happy. I could feel the joy of the inhabitants radiating in waves. Where I came from, we find joy, but it was a joy taken in rising above misery and loss. This was not that. It was pure. It made my heart ache, so I detoured, creeping around it even though I needed food and rest.

Fear drove me onward, longer than it should have, until my feet were numb. I slept a few hours, wracked with uneasy nightmares. The night was still caught in the silver glow of the full moon—a welcome sight I had to bask in for a moment, so unlike our own blood moon—when I woke and continued onward. I still didn't know how I was choosing my path, but there was no uncertainty in where I had to go. Something pulled at me, like when I would run cross country and the path laid itself out in front of me without conscious thought.

About mid-morning, the pines and cedars gave way to the thick grass and broad-shouldered oaks of the foothills. I was traveling more swiftly here, I realized, than I normally would on foot. My path turned south, paralleling the spine of the mountains. This land was very much like my home had been before the wars.

Yet it was bigger. Deadlier. I could taste the teeth in the air, the restless intelligence of the wind. Something was more... alive there. The warmth of the afternoon did nothing to smooth the raised hairs on my arms.

Late in the day, as I walked along the low valley of a saddle back, I saw where my path must be leading me. A great cliff-face loomed ahead, rising from a low valley spotted with gigantic oaks. A river meandered lazily between the trees, and the grass was the beautiful, tawny gold of a mountain-lion's coat. The top of the hill was rough and boulder-strewn, with peculiarly sharp spines here and there.

The sense of *other* was rich and heavy much like the places back home where the gods had risen or now built their lairs, though drier and cleaner.

A thin ridge connected where I stood with where I was heading. Bare of trees or brush, it seemed terribly conspicuous. I felt so utterly alone out there, yet something brooded beneath my feet, warning me of danger.

There was no other way. I would be able to see for miles from the top of that hill, and I thought maybe I could spot a city or whatever was drawing me on. I followed the gentle swell of the hill to the crest and began scrambling along the bare stone.

Under my hands, the rocks were warm, and subtly, beautifully patterned, soft washes of red and pink and white in dark grey.

Finally, the sheer walls widened, and I sat on a great, smooth boulder to catch my breath.

Who can enter my lair? Who sees the broken bridge? Who smells of death and the ending of worlds?

I can still feel the memory of those first thoughts. They were not so much words as impressions on my skin, tastes in my mouth. I knew exactly what has been said, but had no idea how.

"I am from a dark world. I followed a golden light, and what bridge?" The words were out before I actually processed that I hadn't *heard* anything.

Laughter. Again, an impression more than a sound, bright and pleased. *You have just stepped off of the broken bridge, little thing, and there are many dark worlds. Which one do you come from, and why?*

"I come from a world where the stars are gone and the moon is red, where the sun steals color and eats souls. I come from a world where we cannot die and dare not live. I come because I was called."

My words dripped and stank of old magic, bypassing my brain and springing forth in ringing challenge. I swallowed back a surge of power, greater than I'd used since the end of the war, and went on in a less dangerous tone.

"Who are you?" I cried, daring. "If I am little, where are you to be so mighty?"

The stones beneath me shifted, cascades of pebbles bouncing off the cliff toward the valley below. Fearing an avalanche, I tried to scramble clear, but the earth itself was moving.

Look up, little one, and answer your question.

Fear sprang up, some ancestral knowledge of bright teeth gleaming in the dark beyond the safety of fire and weapons. Some awful, towering sense consumed me, like trying to grasp the enormity of a mountain while standing in its shadow. I looked upward, slowly, and gave an involuntary cry, though of fear or awe or longing, I don't know.

A great head lowered toward me, tilting quizzically. Eyes the liquid gold of running water over clean sand examined me. Its fine nostrils, translucent pink in the sun, flared, taking in my scent. A wide streak of white ran down the creature's forehead, stark against the red-washed grey of its hide, veering abruptly to run off its nose, and fine, sharp antlers crowned its head.

"What are you?"

Tsk. You know that answer. Don't ask stupid questions. You might as well ask what you are.

I blushed. "I thought you were fairy tales."

The dragon threw its head back, its long-scaled neck flexing as it roared a very real laugh that shook the trees in the valley.

You come from a world where the gods pass through the veils of reality at will, where empty-eyed people suck the souls from their kin, from a world broken by myth and the cruel results of its choices, and you think I am the fairytale? Oh, child. Ohhhhh, child. I remember now why I have always loved your kind.

I was less pleased by this. It was not my fault that I didn't...no. The dragon was right.

I sighed, admitting as much. "But," I protested, "faith in invisible things is not something we spend much time on these days. We have more visible things to fear than we need."

Faith is foolish, but it is so very human. I wish your people had not lost it. It makes humans beautiful and unpredictable, capable of so many intriguing choices. Mine have not lost their hope or faith. Faith in each other, in the sun, in themselves.

"Your people? There are more like you?"

A few like me, though most are diminished and quiet. But I mean the humans. Some of them are mine, too. Another laugh. It is so human to think that shape is all that matters.

I shrugged. "They are not my people. We are not a people any more. Just a handful of broken survivors."

146

The mental equivalent of a shrug. It did not particularly care what I might think. "Why am I here?"

Our age is ending, the facets you would call worlds are breaking, one by one. It started in one near yours, and now it is rippling through the folds. With every destruction, it grows stronger, the things behind it feeding on the desolation. Your world is not the next, but it is starting to tear. Small horrors are fleeing ahead of the great ones, and good things are fleeing, too, warped by fear and the ripples of hate behind them. If you were able to come here, then something has torn through. The fall of your world is not far behind, then mine, soon after.

"But why was I brought here?"

Were you?

"No one else could see the light."

Another mental shrug. *There are, most likely, others. Maybe slower, maybe faster, maybe somewhere else. The fate of worlds is seldom left to just one being. It's just not wise.*

I laughed. I had to. It was the one thing I'd always hated about the tales my mother raised me on: the chosen one, weight of the world, gets the princess.

It is good that change is coming. Things are too old, and they were broken long ago by my ancestors. It is time for renewal, and somewhere, that renewal was started. Something must have gone wrong, and the destroyers have struggled free.

"Okay, then why am I here?"

Why are you here?

I glared at him. It was surprisingly easy to be annoyed with an ancient, mythical being. At least the part about them talking in riddles and mysteries was true.

"You don't think *I'm* going to do something about gods and monsters and worlds ending?"

Silence.

"Fucking myths."

Another laugh. This was a terribly smug dragon.

You have been lost since you pulled Martin's face from the mud. My knees gave way, pitching me face-first at the rock. A surprisingly gentle hand caught me, cradling me. I'd buried that thought for all the years since the war. Hot bile flooded my throat, choking me.

Be still. His passing was instant and painless, and he died with his eyes on your face. He felt your awful future and his own empty one, and he saved you for it. Something nearly as awful as my own grief slid through those soundless words. *He was a distant child of one of my kin. We felt his loss so greatly, but it was...it was good.*

The scene flooded through me. The mud is red with the blood of our squad. We've been cut off from the platoon and pinned in a small valley for almost two hours. It is a killing field, and only three of us are still alive. We've received word over the radio that help is on the way, seconds before Aaron takes three bullets to the back. Just as we're losing hope, we hear the rest of the platoon arrive and charge forward with renewed fury. Harry pulls the pin on a grenade and tosses it toward a cluster of the enemy.

In an act that should only work in movies, one of them swings her rifle at it and knocks it back to us. Martin shoves me just out of blast range.

Lying there, dazed, while our platoon cleans up the remnants of the enemy, I see Martin's face just beyond me. He looks so peaceful. With a shaking hand, I reach out to touch his forehead. It feels rubbery and soft beneath my fingers, and I scrabble closer to see what is wrong, and it is just his face, just his skin and the top of his skull and his eyes and nothing inside and my hands are sticky with his blood and brains and the rest of him is gone, where is he, Martin Martin Martinmartinmartin--

Cold water splashed over me, and I realized I was screaming with memories, screaming Martin's name. I could still feel that face in my hands. I could remember curling into a ball on the ground, clutching that scrap of death and screaming at the medics to save him.

Another splash. Fury shook me, thinking that the dragon had grown tired of my hysterics. I reared up to scream at it, just as another tear slid off its ridged cheek and splashed into my open mouth. Bitterness exploded across my tongue for a moment, to be replaced with something like rosewater, sweet and old and empty.

I feel your pain child, as you will taste mine in that tear, a little drop of all the tears I have cried over the long centuries. I am sorry, sorry that you have carried this wound for so long without help.

"They sent us to therapists, at first," I said, my voice dull and raw. "They gave us exercises and mantras and pills. Then the therapists went mad, too, and we were just madmen screaming at each other without understanding."

The great beast, ancient myth, god-like thing, cradled me to its chest and let me weep tears that no amount of psychology or drugs had tapped.

Finally, I had no more, and I drew a ragged breath, finding some measure of peace in the vastness of my surroundings and the staggering age and knowledge beside me. There was comfort in my insignificance. I was nothing. There were others. I could curl up on these rocks and watch the ages pass, becoming nothing more than another piece of stone on the hilltop.

If that is what you wish, I will not send you away. You will be cared for here, and loved, and the end will be peaceful.

But I have never been one to lie down and give up. I'd seen too many of the survivors do that, just lie down and fade until they were nothing more than shadows, or their souls died and they rose, empty-eyed and ravenous. The thought ceased to even tempt me. Anger flooded my soul, washing away the memories more cleanly than even the tears. Those were the ones we feared more than the demons or monsters. I would not become like that. A glad madness filled me, a spirit-deep need.

"No," I whispered. "No. No! NO!" I was shouting then, roaring defiance at my despair. Roaring defiance at the gods, at anything that would listen.

A great, wild laugh filled the air, cloaking me in a gown of certainty. The dragon was crying with me again, crying in power and defiance.

Life flooded me for the first time in memory. The taste of roses grew stronger, and I clutched the dragon's horns, pressing myself against its face. "No, I will not go softly into that good night."

Then you will be my champion, and I will give you what you need.

From the dragon's back, I could see the similarities between its world and mine. A great city sprawled on the horizon, shimmering in the evening sun. Broad roads criss-crossed the hills, jammed with cars. *Rush-hour,* I thought, dizzily. They still have enough people to have rush-hour.

We suffered many great wars, but no gods came, no magic. My kin and I diminished and nested in the bones of the earth where we could not be found. We have watched and guarded this place for many long centuries and kept the hungry past away.

"Why do we not have dragons?"

You do. They chose power when we chose survival. They are also bedded in the earth, deeply and to the side of what your eyes can see. Their power is not diminished. It is why I have hope: we are too weak to face the gods, but they...You will call them forth, as perhaps others are calling them, and then we shall see a battle as no other. I wish that I could go with you.

"Why can't you?"

To tear through the folds from this side would only hasten the collapse. I fear we already have too little time.

As we flew, the dragon taught me the history of my world, the things not printed in books. It taught me the weaknesses of gods, the power of mortals, the songs of dragons. It taught me that courage was a mortal thing, and the brilliance of despair. Almost too much, rushing like a river through my mind, until I feared I would drown in it.

All too soon, the flight was over. Full dark had fallen, and as we glided over the tree tops, I could see that golden light again.

There is not enough space for me to land. I must drop you into the water.

Thankfully, I was too mad with knowledge to care. What was a little water, when I held the songs of dragons in my heart?

It turned out that a little water, ice cold, could drive the songs of dragons right out of one's heart. The water had certainly not been this cold when I first came through. The dragon hovered overhead, its great, rocky wings beating with impossible grace. I lifted a shaking hand to assure it I was okay, and, taking a deep breath, dove toward the doorway.

Again, I passed out somewhere on the trip. I woke on the shore of the lake, shivering, with The Ghost standing over me. I scrambled to my feet and hugged him fiercely, thankful that he had not been harmed. We went back to the campsite, and I changed into dry clothes. The dragon's words had made me uneasy, but the world did not seem too different.

The smaller horrors coming through the folds will be hunting the bones of the dragons, my dragon had said. *The greatest changes and distortions will be around their resting place. You have tasted my tears and will know where to find the nearest one.*

"What if there isn't one close to me?" I'd asked.

I can feel him, one of the fire lords. This is a land of flame and eruptions, and he will most likely have nested in the belly of a great volcano.

I knew where that could be. The dragon, before dropping me into the shockingly-cold water, had also given me a talisman, one of its own claws. *Bind this to the mane of your horse, and he will have the strength and speed of a dragon, bearing you where you must go without harm or weariness.*

The long, heavy talon gleamed dully in the moonlight. The Ghost glowed nearly the same hue as he approached and sniffed the thing, but did not seem to disapprove much. His pale eyes flashed as he watched me bind it into his mane, and he stretched his head back to sniff it again, twitching his lip at it. We both felt the magic flood us, and he snorted.

"Steady, steady," I whispered, and pulled myself onto his back. I didn't bother with saddle or bridle. We had become Other, creatures of ancient magic and terrible purpose.

The night flew by us. The same glorious doom infected him, and his bone-white nostrils flared to fuel his great lungs. On and on we ran, until the sun rose over the horizon, and then we could see the dragon's prediction coming true.

Dark shapes moved across the landscape, impossibly vast, a heat-shimmer of strangeness pulling in the world around them. If they were the lesser horrors, then I dreaded to even contemplate the great ones. The air felt thin and cold, and in some places, things blurred and faded as we approached them, as though rubbed out with an eraser.

Something sprawled across the horizon to our left, pulling in great mouthfuls of mountain, chewing through scenery and leaving only emptiness.

We redoubled our efforts and focus. We had to find this lost dragon.

Sometime after noon, we entered the true wilderness, and I became ever more grateful for the talisman. The ground was rocky and steep, and at the speed we were going, The Ghost would have broken a leg without it.

The mountains around us were corpses, black and charred, as though something had set fire to them. The trees were gone and the soil torn away. Great gashes marred the terrain, trenches dozens of feet long. The sky was red with smoke and dust. A black rain started falling, needle-sharp drops staining both of us sooty grey. The Ghost was not used to such weather, and soon thin sores rose on his muzzle and around his eyes. I stopped him for a moment to remove my shirt and form a sort of mask for him. It was not perfect, but we would have to trust the talisman to get us there safely.

Then it was my skin welting under the rain.

Night was falling again when we entered a narrow valley. I slowed The Ghost to a walk. The valley was wooded. Silent. Not even rain intruded into its shelter. We passed herds of deer and wild horses, elk and pronghorn. Yellow eyes gleamed from high branches, where mountain lions, bobcats, raccoons, and squirrels huddled against the branches. Bears, wolves, and coyotes, too. Everything had tried to take refuge here. We were in the right place, I hoped.

Talisman or no, we were weary and wounded, bleeding, panting, soul-sick. My throat was raw from the thin, foul air, a wracking cough shaking me every few minutes. He was a little better, protected by the claw, but blood streamed down his shoulders from grasping branches and the rain. We were sorry heroes, my dirty white steed, and me without even my second-best armor.

Such are the thoughts you think when the world is dying around you and the only possibility of saving...everything...is to wake a dead legend and hope its wrath is enough to stave off the darkest spawn.

A cave-mouth yawned on the cliff in front of us. I stopped at the base, intending to dismount and go alone. The Ghost sidestepped calmly, preventing me from my purpose. His ears were pinned back, and when I paused to see what he was doing, he swung his head to me and gave me a patient, resigned look.

We would finish together. The dragon had taken it for granted that we would, but I had wanted to spare my faithful friend. I buried my face in his sparse mane for a moment, grateful for all the years and hopeless roads and emptiness he had endured with me.

Taking a deep breath, we entered the mountain.

I couldn't tell what was in the cave, or how long we were in there. Sometimes it seemed as though we rushed centuries into the future, at others, that we were diving into the depths of the sea. Perceptions were strange, and I felt the brooding memory of the dragon swirling around me, ready to annihilate me at the least suggestion of danger.

The claw on The Ghost's shoulders glowed bright silver, splashing our shadows against the wall, and suddenly, the walls fell away and we were...there.

Strange light played on a cathedral-like ceiling, hundreds of feet overhead, stalactites glittering in rainbow colors. The floor was perfectly smooth, and I couldn't see the outer walls. The air moved strangely, laden with phantoms and half-seen tableaus.

This was the place.

Leave the claw on your companion, my dragon had said, *and kneel between his front feet. You will both be safe then, from what happens. Touch both palms to the ground and listen. You will know what to do.*

Oh, so easy to believe these things when the sun is bright and the danger only a theory. In the moment, my hands were slick with sweat, and my heart pounded. I followed my instructions, and The Ghost stood perfectly still above me. We were bonded in this, shaman and companion, calling the past, the deep power, the future, the last hope. Not heroes, but voices, embodied prayers, embodied faith. Perhaps I was the soul of my people. Perhaps I was their hope. Or their despair. I had survived all the long years and come to this place on the eve of Armageddon, and I would not fail now.

Then that wild glory filled me again and tore from my throat in a hunting hawk's scream of triumph and defiance. My palms burned, smoking against the ground, but they did not hurt. Shadow and flame fell in great curtains from above us, whispering in the soft susurrus of fine silk. The world heaved and shifted. Furious thrumming drove through my bones, and it seemed the earth itself groaned.

And then...silence. The silence of a held breath, of waiting, expectation.

From those coruscating shadows, something rose. Shadow shifted and eddied, darting here and there to cling to bone. Fire crawled along shadow, melding with it, forming it. We were watching a myth take shape, and it was beautiful.

Finally, a deep shudder wracked the thing, and it shook itself hard, unfolding massive wings that billowed softly in their own wind. I still couldn't see it clearly, only flowing shadows wreathed in flame and smoke. We had found the Fire Lord.

It turned to us. I pressed my face into the sand, and The Ghost's nose pressed against the side of my face. Even he offered respect.

For a long, awful moment, nothing.

I see the ending of the world, and I set myself against it. A drop of something deadly-hot sizzled in the sand before me. *Take my blood and anoint your lips and your steed's hooves with it. Go forth. Call the myths to witness the great defiance of our time and the ending of an age.*

Go, and speak, Faith, speak of what you have seen to the other worlds, to the lost places, and bear my memory with you. I will hold the gates until the armies of the ages can be gathered.

And so we left that place and have come to you. We bear the witness of his sacrifice, and the memory of his glory. We speak for the ancients who stand against Armageddon. We call you, and your kin, to the last war, the war that will determine whether the future will be ruled by horror or great beauty.

By blood and fang and song, we call you.

As the Sun Dies

I DON'T REMEMBER WHAT came before the long night, except as dusty words on a rotting page. Memory has a way of fading, falling to the immediate concerns of life. Survival leaves no room for dreams.

I don't know the names of the rivers we forded. I don't know where we were on that last day, in what country or land we stopped. Our maps were old, stained with fear and hope, pieced together of scraps left from before the fall.

But I remember a song, a prayer, a hope. I remember a misty dream. I remember when we crested that last horizon and the valley spread beneath us, the sun before us. I remember that it was worth every breath, every death, every tear. And there were many of those things.

The world cast us aside, and we found our ties severed, our history erased, our names forgotten. I do not know who will read this song, if anyone has survived the great world-eater who devoured the sun, but I leave this for their hands and hope that it will be sung again in a new earth, that our hope made feed another generation, and that the shining beauty of the old sun not be forgotten forever.

We were alone for so long before the end. The war started in the south and moved through the world like a wildfire, assimilating all the little endless conflicts that have been fought since man first picked up a stone. We were an island in this sea of strife, a town too remote to be strategic, too poor to be useful, too small to be dangerous. So when the infrastructure of the Land of Dreams crumbled, we remained. We were spared the nightmares and madness.

A strange priest or prophet or youngling god found us, now and again. A little nuclear fall-out, a few years of ash-laden rain. We covered our faces, burned the imposters, and filtered our water. When the news networks and internet died, we turned to the wandering traders. By that time, dictators and ghosts and gods ruled the earth; it was just a matter of dividing a ruined world into new nations, so we stopped caring.

As generations passed, we became afraid of the outside. We disappeared from the maps. No one could bother us. We had agreed on this course of action, and no sacrifice was too great. We weaned ourselves from the goods the nomad-traders offered and stopped sending people to the broken cities. If we couldn't make something, we learned to do without. We built a wall, a barrier of denial and traps and broken roads, and rumors were spread of a ruined, cursed town.

We disappeared from the memory of the world, a people unto ourselves.

The clocks slowed, staggered, stilled. Time became meaningless, scored by erratic seasons and faltering days. Those who were young when time stalled never aged, never died. After a while, we stopped noticing.

The nights became shorter, lighter, until the sun caught in our sky and baked our fields to ash. The rivers dried, and lakes shrank, until the weather patterns shifted again and storms snarled in from the broken coasts of the west. The stones in the hills steamed when the first drops hit, and our houses seemed to breathe again as the dust washed from them. The streams ran like red milk.

We became used to the changing of things, to unpredictability. We survived whatever was thrown in our path, and we wandered along a path into eternity, not doubting that we would surmount any challenge.

But our peace betrayed us, blinded us to the slow winding of the spindle, and when we saw it, it was too late. The end didn't come quietly. When the earthquakes hit, three houses fell into a crack across the South River neighborhood. For days, the ground heaved beneath us, and our dead moaned in their graves.

By the end of the week, it was dark, and morning hadn't come for three days. A thick gloom choked the streets, not smoke or fog or dust, but some creeping darkness that shrouded lights and smothered voices into whispers. Strange, white lights glimmered in the sky, but they were not stars, not machines, and their glow was brief and malevolent.

We thought it would go away. For days, weeks, months, we hoped. The sun was not gone. We could not accept it, as if our faith would bring it back. The new gods were not powerful enough to change the universe itself; they were figments of man's wickedness and imagination. So we sat in the darkness and prayed to the old gods, prayed that our willful disregard could somehow restore our world.

Winter settled on the mountains, and then the plains. Snow buried our houses, until we had to dig tunnels to reach our neighbors. We became a subterranean people. We slaughtered most of our animals and preserved the meat; we were used to preparing for hardship, our supplies were stocked and we went on short rations. Our men dug long tunnels onto the plains to bring back dead trees and harvest the dead grass for the few beasts we kept. We took turns watching the sky from the town square, the only place we could keep clear of the snow and ice.

Finally, we gave in to reality. The sun wasn't returning. We were running out of food and running out of soul. We found an old HAM radio in an attic. We figured out how to operate it, eventually, and sent our voices out.

Months passed. We despaired, gave up on the sun and on our kin.

And then, word came. It flew from halfway around the world, bounced from city to village to town to hermit to settlement to us. *The world doesn't spin anymore. The world is dark in one land, burning in another. Something woke up, it is eating the sun. The old gods are too busy warring to notice.*

We cried like children who have lost their parent, until anger drove into our hearts and defiance dried our tears. We threw open every switch and flooded the town with our precious energy, blazing our light into the night. *We are going to find the sun, to witness for its fall,* we said, and sent a call across the air. *Join us. We are the children of the old earth, of fire and madness and joy. Join us.*

They came, trudging over the ice with their ragged possessions and scrawny children. We opened dusty old buildings for them to sleep in. One by one, they gathered to us with their worldly goods and hopes and their mending dreams.

And on every tongue, the joyful news. *The sun lives. The world has shifted. The sun lives in the south.*

So we packed up our lives and our goods. Our children and starving animals came with us, and behind us, only ghosts and unlocked doors remained, flapping in the roaring winds. We would not return. Let the birds and beasts make caves of our dwellings, let them try to survive in the ice and wind.

We pointed our cold-cracked compasses south by southwest, toward the sea.

There were so many miles, so many mountains and hills and endless deserts, rock and ice and roaring rivers barring us from our goal. Ruined cities loomed, the rusting hulks of skyscrapers and collapsing tenements hiding evils we had never known. The worst of the destruction had centered on the cities, where pale-eyed humans slipped through the shadows like feral cats, baring their fangs if we approached. The clinging night was filled with the cry of hunter and prey, and great, unseen things swept us with their wind as they passed over, sometimes snatching one of our number. We passed walled enclaves, ringed with fire and razor wire, guarded by sharp-eyed hunters who did not turn their faces to us, or open their gates.

Sometimes we saw the new gods moving across the landscape, their beautiful, impossible monstrosities blacking out the stars or sliding across the ruins like oozing tar. We avoided those, cowering in shadows from a creature that loomed like a skyscraper, its whirring eyes limned with a soft blue glow, running aside from a many-legged thing that rooted through steel girders to find the dog-sized cockroaches that sometimes scuttled across our path, tossing them into the air and devouring them whole. There was even a slithering, hissing thing of cords and chips, glowing red and green from a thousand blinking eyes.

But these were not interested in us and, as long as we kept watch, were no danger. We lost many more to the small, quick spirits, with their gleaming razors and plastic eyes. They came and were gone in a spray of blood or a truncated scream.

Finally, the cities fell behind us, and we found ourselves in cold deserts. Dozens of us died, and, our supplies depleted, we drank their blood like beasts, used their raw hides to mend our tattered shoes and clothes.

We climbed into the mountains again—mountains taller and crueler than those before—and felt the first tendrils of warmth beneath our feet. For weeks, we traveled, worn to thin shadows of ourselves, hard and hungry for the light, and finally, a glorious cry rose from the front of the line as our leaders crested the last mountain.

Huge and brooding, the sun rested on the horizon, weary prey fleeing for safety. Above us, the light gleamed on the scales of a vast, terrible serpent, casting its shadow across the valley below, its scales white as rotting flesh.

The light painted our tears as blood, and we looked like corpses. So long in the cold, in the dark and the cloud-shrouded stars that we had forgotten heat and light. We shielded our eyes and wiped sweat from our faces.

Someone started singing, crooning a wordless lullaby. A man, one of our preachers, hummed a dirge. A woman's voice lifted in a wild tangent, grief and joy mingling. One by one, we all started singing our own songs, minor melodies blending into a great paean.

Tears and song and light and dust mingled together as the sun slowly sank beneath the horizon and clouds stole across the sky, pushed by that great hunter.

I sank to the ground, clutching my knees to my chest. It was so short. Was this it? No more? The sun was gone, though the rumors said the world was still. Did we pick up and climb again? The sea loomed on the horizon. Where could we go? Would the sun return, or would the serpent swallow it first?

We had nothing left. Our packs were emptied and discarded along the trail, our clothes worn to rags. We had only the pride of survival.

We found that maybe we did remember something after all.

We had laughed and loved and cried. We lived a dozen lifetimes under that starred sky. If we didn't remember the seconds of them, what does it matter? I'd learned that memory isn't the half of it. It might only be a luminescent, quiet softness deep in my soul that told me of that eternity of darkness and travel. It was enough, I never had that softness in my soul in the old days.

And we had found the sun.

"We climb no more mountains," I cried. "We stay! The sun has blessed this spot, and this is where we will make our last stand and wait! It will return!"

So we found shelter in the rocks. We scavenged sticks and mud and made little houses for ourselves. Those who were too weak to build sat and wove dry grass into mats for roof and floor. Children ran to and fro, bring arm-loads of grass, buckets of water. The strong mixed the clay and grass and water into a thick muck, and we smoothed it over the rough structures. It would have to be enough, but it used up everything we had.

We were without strength. Everything had been given to the sun, and without it, we faded. Our mud-crusted bodies ached with grief and exhaustion. We huddled under the skeletons of our buildings, muck dripping on us. Nothing dried, rot and mold crept through everything.

Mud and dust and decay in our mouths and noses, our fingers bleeding in the darkness, it was misery we had never known, even in the ice. No one laughed. No one sang. No children were conceived. Our numbers fell again as madness and starvation and despair claimed the weak.

When that long night ended and the hulking sun rose again, it burned through the clouds and the huts baked. Animals woke from their lethargy and began to mate and hunt. All work was put aside. We bathed in the cold, clear water of the river and watched it run red to the red sun on the red horizon. After the bleak night, we basked in the color, but always behind it was the sinister length of the monster, slow and inexorable as a glacier.

We stripped our stinking clothes off and tossed them into the river. The village glowed with a macabre beauty, and we danced as though possessed by the sun itself. The serpent's scales reflected the sun in glittering rainbows now; its fangs dripped venom that ate through mountains and boiled the sea, and we prayed that it did not fall on our broken village.

Then, the sun set again as we clustered in the square and wept. We had no way to mark the passage of time. The beasts crept close to us, scenting our huddled bodies and our fear.

We crafted weapons to defend ourselves. Crude spears and bows and arrows that flew crookedly while the ravens mocked us. The rabbits ignored everything we did to catch them. Deer watched us until we were almost on them, and then strolled off as we hobbled after them.

In our hunger, we ate the earth for its minerals, the grass like dumb cattle. Our bellies grew distended and our teeth fell out. The children, conceived in the sun, died as they were born in the dark.

Suddenly, after another eternity, there was light on the horizon and the sun rose again. We gathered what food we could. Better weapons were made, slings of animal hide and dead wood, clubs, stone knives. We made new traps for rabbits and birds, we sewed what clothes and blankets we could, and raised more houses. We built a great drum so that we would know how long the night lasted.

We would live through the next night, and we did.

It was enough.

But each night grew longer, each day shorter, and darker. The clouds no longer fled the sun, but dared to drift across his face and cast yet more shadows on us, drawn by the breath of the monster. The drum beat, day and night, but the nights were longer than the days, and with every day, the serpent's fangs were closer to the dimming bulk of the bright star.

Our hearts despaired, but we were strong now, and we gathered in the fading days and sang wild songs, glorious songs, glad songs to the sun, as if we could strengthen his flight.

And then we saw the great sun shrinking. Each day, he was smaller. Each day he sank sooner, like a tired old man, and his pursuer took heart. The gap closed.

The crimson light faded and the shadows deepened, each day colder and darker, until the red sun was little more than a dull glow on the horizon and color leached out of the world, out of our bright hair and our dyed clothing.

As the days faded, the nights lengthened and color disappeared, we sang a little louder, we danced a little harder. It wasn't praise of the red sun by then. It was furious defiance of his hunter, as those distended jaws began to engulf the sun, light glowing through its swollen skin. The serpent's eyes, as vast as cities, threw off a cold white light, usurping the red.

Days were barely tinged here and there with a pale red glow. We, the old ones, put aside our tools, our weapons and our duties, and sat in vigil to this great death.

Our singers offered slow reveries as our blood thickened in our veins. So attuned to the sun, we faded with him. Our songs grew softer, weaker. We no longer needed to eat, nor to drink.

Those who had been born after—who had not followed the sun on that great trek across the world—did not wish to die with us. So they moved us outside of the village, and as the sun died, they dug our graves and set us within. We were forgotten, and civilization built around us, a great, white city, its murals drawn in shades of charcoal and chalk and dried blood.

The drum beat slowly through the long nights. Boom boom boom boom, a heartbeat that settled into our blood and bones. Our hearts met that rhythm.

The red sun rose again, laboring towards the horizon. There was no glorious painted light anymore. His dull fire bled down the serpent's throat. This would be the final day.

The drum echoed across the world. *Boom.*

Our hearts told us so, the smell of scorched god-child told us so.

Thoom

Our slowing blood told us so, our grief told us so.

161

Thoom

Chants slowed, our voices deepened, each of us humming our own note, melting into a grief-stricken hymn.

Thoom

The pale-eyed young, not wishing to die, stuffed their ears with grass.

Thoom

The creatures of the plain came to us, mountain lion and coyote. Raven and crow. Rabbit and serpent.

Thoom

Ranks of them. Lion and lamb together to witness to the end of an age.

Thoom

Long and slow into that final night, the sun sank towards the horizon. We lay in our graves, our eyes fixed to that dim great giant.

Thoom

A coyote cried its weirding song, other creatures joining in countermelody to our voices.

Thoom

Thoom

Thoom

And now the drum beat is nearly gone. This night will never end. The sun is a glow of red from the mouth of a world-eater, its blood mingling with the serpent's venom and falling in an acid rain.

Does our blood still flow? Does it still pound through our hearts? We can't tell. All is silent. Heavy, greasy anticipation.

Waiting.

Our breath slows.

It is time. His last light is fading. We are fading. My sight blurs.

I don't know how many years we wandered. I don't remember how many mountains we climbed.

I don't remember the faces of my kin and companions. I don't remember my own past-name, or my childhood.

But I remember ghosts. I remember a song, a prayer, a hope. I remember a misty dream. I remember when we crested that last horizon and the valley spread beneath us. I remember that it is worth every breath, every death, every tear.

The animals whimper, pressing their bellies to the earth. Their eyes are fixed on the horizon.

Light blooms one last time, a tidal wave of red and gold, and the serpent thrashes in panic as heat sweeps the earth.

Thoom.

Dreams...end

MY FINGERS BRUSH THE last page to its rest. The libraries rest in my memory now, but I have no one to pass the stories to. They have all given themselves to hold back the Light a little longer so that I might commit the last pages to memory. I am alone.

A chamber waits with open arms, filled with sorcery thick as oil and restless as the sea. The Light presses against my temples and sears my skin from my bones. It turns the myths to ash, their beautifully-scribed words fading instantly. We were the last who held out, the only ones strong enough to hold back the Light, to hope that when nothing remained to cast a shadow, the Light would fade.

The last book crumbles beneath my fingers, and I sink into the chamber's depths. The sorcery is already reacting to the Light, the crests of its waves hissing and smoking. It is of the night, and the Light reaches for it hungrily. The thick waves close over my face, and it is only with the tenacity born of long discipline that I am able to hold still as it swarms into my brain and lungs.

The Light closes over me, sinks its teeth into the Night that enfolds me, and the universe blinks out in silence...

Jaym Gates

41828287R10105

Made in the USA
Middletown, DE
25 March 2017